2574

F
FOS   Foster, John T.

                 The gallant gray
                 trotter

DATE DUE

THE GALLANT GRAY TROTTER

Books by John T. Foster

THE GALLANT
GRAY TROTTER

JOHN T. FOSTER

ILLUSTRATED BY SAM SAVITT

DODD, MEAD & COMPANY
NEW YORK

ISBN: 0-396-06869-3
Library of Congress Catalog Card Number: 73-11988
Printed in the United States of America

For my aunt, Bernadine McLaughlin,
who has dedicated her life to books,
this book is dedicated with love
and appreciation

ACKNOWLEDGMENTS

Did people use such-and-such an expression back then? What did they eat in those days? What did they wear?

These are some of the problems facing the writer of a novel laid in the past. The answer to the problems is research and luck. This writer was lucky enough to have use of the services of the Suffolk County Bookmobile staff and Carleton Kelsey of the Amagansett Free Library. From them, I received most of my historical information and material on the Montauk Indians.

They also found for me the John Hervey biography of Lady Suffolk, *Lady Suffolk, the Old Gray Mare of Long Island*, and *The Trotting Horse of America: How to Train and Drive Him, with Reminiscences of the Trotting Turf*, by Hiram Woodruff, published in 1874. Woodruff, the foremost trainer and driver of his day, competed against Lady Suffolk many times. His book is a gold mine of tips, anecdotes, and racetrack color.

I would also like to acknowledge the expert information

supplied me by Stanley F. Bergstein, Vice President, publicity-public relations, United States Trotting Association; Philip A. Pines, Director, Hall of Fame of the Trotter, Goshen, New York; Edwin T. Keller, President, American Harness Racing Secretaries, Inc.; Ken McCarr; and Dr. John C. Stevenson.

Finally, I found Currier and Ives lithographs extremely helpful. The two did many illustrations of Lady Suffolk, showing in fine detail the American scene in those "merry old times that are gone."

CONTENTS

CONTENTS

AUTHOR'S NOTE

Much of this story is true. It is based upon the life of Lady Suffolk, the most famous trotting horse in the world during her period. Lady Suffolk was born in Smithtown, Suffolk County, Long Island, New York, in the spring of 1833, and died in Bridport, Vermont, on March 7, 1855. Her great-grandsire was Messenger, the gray English stallion that is the foundation sire of all modern American trotters. (Messenger, incidentally, is buried in Locust Valley on Long Island, where a bronze plaque in his memory can be seen.)

Lady Suffolk is probably the only racehorse ever to have had a song written about her. In her declining years, the tune, "The Old Gray Mare," appeared and promptly became a hit, its popularity lasting to the present day. In fact, even the wooden horses used today as models for harness goods are gray, in honor of Lady Suffolk.

During her career of sixteen seasons, Lady Suffolk participated in 162 races, winning 89, and coming in second in 56. She was the first horse in history to trot the mile in less than $2\frac{1}{2}$ minutes—the equivalent of Roger Bannister running the mile under four minutes in 1954.

Although they are in accord that Lady Suffolk was the first horse to break the $2\frac{1}{2}$-minute mile, historians disagree upon exactly when and where she did it. John Hervey, who devoted a full biography to the horse, *Lady Suffolk, the Old Gray Mare of Long Island*, says the event took place at the Centreville Course on Long Island on September 24, 1840. Her time: 2:29. She later trotted the mile under $2\frac{1}{2}$ minutes in a number of races, which is, perhaps, the reason for the confusion.

As the real Lady Suffolk continued to race, her fame grew until people all over northeastern United States flocked to see her, caring little whether she won or lost.

Lady Suffolk's achievements are the more extraordinary in view of the fact that this small mare wore shoes weighing a pound or more apiece, compared to the modern trotter's shoes of three or four *ounces* each. Today the racing sulky weighs 27 pounds. The ones Lady Suffolk pulled were in the 50- to 60-pound range. To achieve her record, the little gray mare from Long Island traveled through seventeen states, almost always pulling her own sulky and her owner-driver behind her.

Lady Suffolk developed her tremendous power by drawing a heavily loaded butcher's wagon around Long Island. Then a livery stable owner bought her for use as a workhorse. Upon the advice of a pair of sports writers who had witnessed her speed, the owner began to race her. At the peak of her career, Lady Suffolk was nearly burned to death in a stable fire.

In spite of constant harsh treatment and scant rest between the events, she never gave anything but her best in every race. She became famous for her great strength, endurance, and pluck.

So then, the Lady Suffolk of my story is closely modeled upon the real horse, and many of the events described in this book are as they actually occurred. No human character, however, is patterned after any real person.

John T. Foster
Montauk, Long Island, New York

THE GALLANT GRAY TROTTER

1

INTO THE UNKNOWN

Fall came to Long Island early that year. The grass of the pasture on the Joshua Desmond farm began to turn brown in September. With their vivid red and yellow leaves, the trees seemed to have burst into flame. When the leaves drifted to the ground, they scratched along in the wind like tiny animals. At first, one of them was enough to send the gray filly on a wild race around the pasture. Gradually, she grew used to the leaves—but still broke into a gallop at the sight of one, leaping about, just for the fun of it. The two Desmond cows watched her with their big, brown, drowsy eyes, then went on chewing their cud.

The filly was on such a romp one nippy morning when her mother nickered to her from the other side of the pasture. Then Tecumseh, young Josh Desmond's brown and white collie, came rushing toward her, barking. She had no fear of him, but she galloped off, with Tecumseh at her heels, because that was fun, too. Now on one side, then on the other, he escorted her back to the barnyard.

Standing by the chicken coop as she came pounding up were Josh, his father, and another man. He was extremely tall and thin, with a clay-red, deeply lined face, fringed with a wispy black beard, and he had sunken blue eyes that seemed to be peering out from twin caves, under eyebrows like bushes. He had a long, black buggy whip that he kept flexing in his white-gloved hands as he stared at the filly.

"So this is the great-granddaughter of Messenger," the stranger remarked. His voice was little more than a whisper.

"Right," Mr. Desmond answered. "You can see she has his gray coat."

"Doesn't appear she got anything else from him, though, does it?" the other man asked. "Look at those big ears. Look at those crimpy little hoofs. She'll never stand more than fifteen hands when she's full-grown."

"She's a good, sound horse, with excellent teeth and bone structure," Mr. Desmond told him firmly. "She'd make a fine mount for some young man."

"If Messenger was her *great*-grandsire, who was her grandsire?"

"Engineer."

"Engineer," the man repeated, pulling his beard thoughtfully. "Wasn't there some mystery about his origin? Seems to me I heard something . . ."

"There was a story that Engineer came to Canada from England during the Great War," Mr. Desmond said.

"The one you were in," his son broke in.

"Right," his father replied. "Engineer was supposed to have been ridden by some British general who was shot off his back in a battle with our troops at Ontario, in 1814.

[18]

The horse wandered into the American lines. Someone captured him and brought him to Long Island. That's the story. I've never believed it."

"Might be some truth in it, after all," the other man said. *"Something's* funny in that filly's background. She looks more like a mule than a horse to me."

"Then you're not interested in buying her?" Mr. Desmond asked with some impatience.

"I didn't say that, now. Bill Billings is always interested in horseflesh. Bill Billings has been buying and selling horseflesh in the state of New York for these past thirty years, so he should know something about the subject. To me, she looks more like a mule than a horse, but I could be wrong. They say the man who is his own attorney has a fool for a client."

"Make me an offer," Mr. Desmond said. He was a large, heavy-set man in boots and overalls, with sandy hair going gray at the temples, a big square face peppered with freckles, and a nose like a plow.

"I'll make you an offer," the horse dealer replied. "Fifty dollars American."

"You'll have to do much better than that," Mr. Desmond told him. "And we're talking about hard money—no shinplasters."

"Hard money, of course," Billings agreed. "I've always said gold and silver are the best currency for a republic. The one thing right that military despot in Washington City has done is to attack the United States Bank and its paper money, yes, sir."

"That 'military despot' won the war," Mr. Desmond pointed out quietly.

"Don't misunderstand me, sir," the dealer quickly replied. "Bill Billings takes nothing away from Old Hickory, no siree. 'Huzza for Old Hickory,' says I. Jackson did indeed win the war, he did indeed—with the help of a few thousand stout lads such as yourself. I wanted to go, I wanted desperately to go, but I was too old—aye, too old. Oh, it was a sad day for Bill Billings when the men in the village marched off to war, with the flags flying, and the drums beating and the fifes playing 'Hail Columbia'. . . . Fifty-five dollars."

"Still much too low," Mr. Desmond told him.

"Anyhow, that horse is going to be a champion some day," Josh said. Like his father, he was dressed in boots and overalls and, eleven years old, was a small replica of Mr. Desmond, even to the plow-like nose.

"Champion of what?" the dealer asked in his whispery voice.

"I don't know," Josh admitted. "I just know she's going to be a champion."

"What's her name?"

"Lady Suffolk," Josh told him.

"Oh, because she was born here in Suffolk County," Billings said. "Well, let's have a look at you, Lady Suffolk."

The filly shifted her weight nervously as the dealer pulled her mouth open to examine her teeth. He stared into her big, clear eyes, then ran his hands up and down her legs and all over her strong, young body. Finally, he picked up her hoofs, one by one, and studied them.

"Very well," Billings said at last, "what do you want for her?"

"One hundred dollars."

"Seventy."

"Never."

"Papa, let's keep her," Josh urged.

"No, son, we've got to sell her," his father replied, "although not necessarily to Mr. Billings here. We have debts that must be paid. A deputy sheriff's compensation doesn't stretch very far."

"You're a deputy sheriff?" the horse dealer asked in his small voice. "Seventy-five dollars."

"Ninety-five," Mr. Desmond replied.

"Eighty."

"Ninety-five," Mr. Desmond repeated.

"Ninety dollars American, and not a penny more!"

"Sold!"

"Oh!" Josh exclaimed.

To seal the bargain, the two men shook hands. Then Billings reached deep into his pocket and pulled out a worn, leather pouch. With some difficulty because of his gloves, he loosened the thong, then, aloud, counted out ninety dollars in clinking silver.

"As our own Senator Marcy has said, 'To the victor belong the spoils,' " the horse dealer remarked.

Mr. Desmond smiled. "You have a good buy there and you know it."

"Well, every man must go to the devil by his own road," Billings replied. Then he leaned forward and spoke in a low voice. "Listen, now, sir, as a personal favor, kindly oblige me and don't tell anyone you managed to get Bill Billings to give you ninety dollars for this horseflesh. If you do, I'm ruined, sir, ruined!"

Mr. Desmond snorted.

"Now, then, Lady Suffolk," the dealer said, "by your leave." Before the filly knew what was happening, the man had slipped a noose over her head. Wobbling from a bad limp, he started for his buggy, pulling her behind him. She fought the rope, rearing up on her hind legs and neighing in terror.

The dealer laughed merrily. "No need to get upset, girl," he told her. "Nobody's going to get hurt, nobody. My, but you're a stubborn one, though. You put me in mind of that half-blood of mine. I'm looking forward to introducing you to Little Billy."

He tied the rope to the rear axle, then climbed into the buggy, ordering, "Go ahead, Waterloo."

The horse, an old bay gelding with a white forehead and four white stockings, started forward, the vehicle rumbling behind him, pulling the filly. She gave a long, forlorn whinny, calling to her mother, who answered in the same way.

Over the rumble of wheels and thudding of hoofs, the filly heard another sound—the patter of running feet. Josh Desmond was chasing after her. Billings gave him a merry wave, then clicked his tongue, and the gelding increased his speed. Josh did his best to keep up, but quickly fell behind.

"Good-by, Lady Suffolk!" he called. "You're going to be a champion some day. I just know it. Good-by, Lady Suffolk!"

The filly caught a glimpse of the boy as the road curved, but then it curved back the other way, and she lost sight of him. Finally, Josh's voice died out. The horse dealer glanced over his shoulder, then brought the whistling whip

down on the back of the gelding with a sharp crack. Waterloo broke into a brisk trot, and the filly had to go along as best she could, each hoofbeat taking her farther from the life she had loved and into the unknown.

2

A BOY CALLED DOG

The winding dirt road was deeply rutted by the wheels of buggies and wagons, which made traveling difficult. Puddles reflected the leaden sky, and the water was cold on the filly when she splashed through one.

From far behind them sounded a trumpet blast. *Er-r-r-rah, er-r-r-rah!*

Billings glanced over his shoulder and Lady Suffolk saw a look of rage that twisted his face, making it redder yet. He laid on the whip, and Waterloo shot forward, jerking the noose around the filly's neck. They mounted a hill, then plunged down a deep descent, to rumble along a corduroy road of logs stretched over a swampy area.

Er-r-r-rah, er-r-r-rah! Ta-ta-tah!

The trumpet sounded much closer. The horse dealer plied the whip. They were approaching a hamlet. Smoke rose from the big brick chimneys of the little frame houses. Squealing pigs scurried out of their path. Chickens, squawking in terror, flew to safety. Barking dogs charged after them, snapping at the horses' fetlocks. Behind her, the filly heard the thudding of many hoofs and the rumble of wheels. Billings whipped the old bay repeatedly, but could get no greater speed out of him.

The thudding and rumble grew steadily louder. Then Lady Suffolk saw two horses in harness, abreast, coming up fast from behind. They passed her and another pair quickly appeared, then a stagecoach, swaying in its bull-hide sling.

The driver, who wore a black stovepipe hat and flapping gray cloak, stared straight ahead, ignoring the buggy as if it weren't there, tooting on his long horn. But a mud-spattered man riding in the stage stuck his head out the window and yelled at Billings, "You can't beat us, sir! Nothing can, and that's a fact!"

The horse dealer was speechless in his rage. The stagecoach rumbled by and drew up at a way station, where a fresh driver and team were waiting. Billings drove on past. . . . Then, in a very short while, *Er-r-r-rah, er-r-r-rah* again sounded, and the stage thundered by a second time. The new driver, also in the gray cloak and stovepipe hat that were the symbols of his office, was just as arrogantly oblivious of the buggy as his predecessor had been.

"You see, sir?" the passenger shouted to Billings. He withdrew for a moment, then his happy, muddy face popped out again. "Sir, we average ten miles an hour for the whole trip, and that's a fact!"

The swaying stage passed on. Only when it had vanished did the horse dealer let up on the pace he was trying to set with Waterloo—and then not much.

Lady Suffolk was nearing the point of exhaustion. Her

hoofs felt over-sized and iron-heavy. Her heart was hammering as if it would crash through her rib cage. From his labored breathing, Waterloo was also on the verge of collapse.

The road, corduroy again, meandered through a dark wood—stumps, rotting logs, stunted trees with gnarled, mossy limbs, and great pools of stagnant green water. The buggy wheels drummed over the logs with a muffled rumble. Each hoofbeat shot pain up the filly's legs. She was beginning to stumble. Then daylight shone ahead and they were out of the wet forest and into open country.

There appeared a broken stone wall on the left; and, when they came to a warped gate in it, Waterloo halted of his own accord. Billings stepped down, opened the squealing gate, then closed it after them when they had passed through. They went crunching up a narrow path paved with clam shells to a dilapidated barn across from a shabby little farmhouse. The horse dealer was hollering before they entered the barnyard.

"Dog! Get out here. You hear me, Dog?"

A tall, bony woman with long blond hair came to the back door of the farmhouse, drying her big red hands on her apron. "Mr. Billings," she yelled, "will you kindly oblige me by not shouting!"

"Mrs. Eller," the dealer replied, "it would please me if you got back to the kitchen where you belong. Dog! Where is that worthless half-blood? Dog!"

"He was here a minute ago," the housekeeper said. "Stephen? There he is!"

A slim, broad-shouldered boy, with reddish-brown skin and straight black hair, was standing at the end of the barn.

He was wearing patched woolen trousers, a ragged buck-skin hunting shirt, and moccasins. He gazed solemnly and silently at the horse dealer with unblinking eyes that were as blue as a summer sea. His thin, sharp-featured face looked as though he had never smiled in his life.

"Why didn't you come when I called you?" Billings demanded.

"My name isn't Dog," the boy replied.

"It is to me."

"My name is Stephen Seven Trees."

"That's your Indian name. To me, you're Dog because you don't talk any more than one hardly. You understand?"

Stephen made no reply.

"Do you understand, Dog?"

The boy remained silent. Lady Suffolk snorted and pawed the ground nervously, sensing the tension in the air.

Jumping down from the buggy, the horse dealer limped over to Stephen, who made no attempt to escape. Billings swung a long arm, cuffing him on the side of the head. The boy staggered and almost fell, but uttered no sound. The man swung his other arm and sent Stephen sprawling.

"Mr. Billings!" the woman yelled, coming out onto the swaybacked porch. "Leave the boy be! The way you treat him is an abomination. And he your own flesh and blood!"

"Not my flesh and not my blood," the horse dealer replied. He was making a strong effort to collect himself, breathing deeply.

"Well, he's your sister's son."

"I was only working on the Indian part," Billings said dryly.

"What's wrong with you?" she asked. "You come in here like a dozen goblins are after you, with two horses you've run nearly to death, and then you start beating Stephen for no good reason. Have you gone mad?"

"That's next kin to nonsense," the horse dealer replied, still taking deep breaths.

"Something must have started you. . . . Oh, I know what! You tried conclusions with another stage and lost. Aren't I correct?"

There was a long pause, during which the only sound was the snorting of Lady Suffolk and the bay. Then Billings shrugged his narrow shoulders, smiling as well as he could. "Yankees are reckoned to be considerable of a go-ahead people."

"Listen now, I'm a Yankee, too," Mrs. Eller replied. "But I don't get transformed into a maniac whenever I set eyes on a stage. I believe you are a little exalted in the head on that subject."

"You think you know so much, madam, when you actually know so little. 'A man who is his own attorney has a fool for a client'—and that extends to women, too."

"Yes?"

"Yes."

"I expect it's more than just wanting to win a race, although everybody seems to be suffering from Fetlock Fever these days," the housekeeper told him. "You truly hate stages, and there must be some reason for that. I wonder what it is. Did you fall off one when you were in Tennessee? They're forever tipping over."

"Don't trouble your head, madam, don't trouble your head." The dealer turned to Stephen Seven Trees, who had picked himself up and was exchanging a long look with Lady Suffolk.

"Dog, I would take it as a kindness if you would look to the filly," Billings said with heavy sarcasm. "I'll manage the bay. Water her out first. Then give her a good grooming—by which I mean don't just dab at her. Put some strength into it—and then let her have some dinner. Put her in the stall next to Waterloo."

Stephen walked forward lightly. He was straight but not stiff, his arms swinging loosely from his shoulders. He untied the rope from the buggy axle, then approached Lady Suffolk. If she hadn't felt so sore and tired, she would have been skittish with the stranger. But, the way it was, she acted as docilely as Waterloo, although she snorted a few times.

Reaching up slowly, Stephen patted her on the neck until she stopped snorting. Then he led her around the barn to a long stone trough filled with water—cool, refreshing water. As she was drinking, he slipped a blanket over her. When she had taken several mouthfuls—but long before she was satisfied—he pulled her gently away and began to walk her in the pasture.

After several minutes, he led her back to the trough and let her drink again. He alternated the drinking and walking until she had drunk her fill. Nearby, the dealer was doing the same with Waterloo, although not so gently.

After Lady Suffolk was watered out, Stephen led her back to the barn, slipped off the blanket and rope, and began to run a comb through her coat. He worked in circles, moving from her head to her tail. Then he gave her a good brushing. Each stroke relaxed her more and stimu-

lated the flow of blood through her body until she tingled.

She was ready for her dinner when Stephen brought the hay and then the oats to her stall. Both were rather moldy and not very pleasant to taste, but Stephen was unaware of the fact and Lady Suffolk was hungry. She cleaned up the manger.

Besides Waterloo and herself, there were three other horses in the barn. As the afternoon wore on, the soft sounds of tails swishing, hoofs thumping in the straw, and noses sniffling in mangers made her drowsy. She was almost dozing when the dealer slipped up to her stall.

3

LITTLE BILLY

"Now then, Lady Suffolk," Billings whispered. "Let us have a training session."

He slipped the rope over her head and, opening the door of her stall, led her through the barn. As the dealer passed Waterloo's stall, the bay gave a deep, bellowing neigh. The other horses were snorting and stamping. The filly, affected by their nervousness, began to balk.

"You're not acting very ladylike, Lady Suffolk," Billings remarked, with a sharp yank on the rope. He dragged her outside, her hoofs plowing furrows in the dirt, and tied her to a post.

"I believe it's time you met Little Billy," the dealer told her. "Little Billy, this is Lady Suffolk. Give her a kiss, eh? 'That I'll do gladly,' says Little Billy."

There was a quick swishing in the air, and then a loud crack and, for the first time in her life, the filly experienced agony. It was so intense that it seemed to cover her entire body. Neighing in pain and terror, she reared, paw-

ing the air with her forelegs. But the rope held, the noose choking her.

"It appears she likes your kisses, Little Billy," the dealer said. "Give her some more, eh?"

The terrible whip came down four more times, raising long welts on the filly's back and sides. Her knees were beginning to buckle and she couldn't get enough air. The dealer, himself, was puffing from exertion.

The door banged open as Mrs. Eller rushed out onto the porch. "Mr. Billings!" she shouted. "What on earth are you doing to that little horse?"

"It would appear to anyone with eyes in his head that I'm giving her a few stripes," the dealer replied.

"Why?"

He took a deep breath. "If it's any concern of yours—which I doubt—I am teaching Lady Suffolk her first lesson in the Bill Billings System. And the subject of this lesson, Mrs. Eller, is who is the master—the man or the horse? If the horse understands that the man is master, she will make a good horse. If she thinks that she's the master, she'll make a very poor horse indeed, and the man might as well give up trying to teach her anything else because she'll refuse to learn."

"But why do you have to whip her?"

"I am punishing her, madam, for fighting me. When she does what I want her to, I will reward her. That, madam, is the way the Bill Billings System works. Bad—Little Billy. Good—an apple, carrot, or lump of sugar. Billings has used this program to break in hundreds of horses, and used it successfully, madam, *used it successfully, madam.*"

Lady Suffolk stood quivering with terror. The whip cuts

still hurt, only a little more than the rope burn around her neck, but at least she could breathe now. She noticed Stephen Seven Trees standing by the barn, where he had been the first time she saw him. He was gazing at her steadily. It was as though he had never moved.

"I know the Billings System is successful," the housekeeper replied. "I've seen you break in a nation of horses, but why do they have to be *broken?*"

"Mrs. Eller," the dealer said, "we have plowed up this same identical ground before, but when you ask me why does a horse have to be broken, you are talking like a steamboat lawyer. You are talking like a stagecoach attorney. *Broken* and *trained* are one and the same, madam; synonymous terms, madam; *synonymous terms, madam.*"

"But she's such a young horse. I believe a little kindness—"

"Kindness, madam?" Billings interrupted. "Kindness is fine at the proper time and in the proper place. In training a horse, however, the mischief springs from too much kindness. The horse don't appreciate it. He's a humbug. You show him too much kindness and not enough of Little Billy here, and he's utterly useless. I repeat, madam, utterly useless."

"Do tell! But what good is he if he's dead?"

The sun was setting behind horizontal cloud bars of red and blue, and the shadows of the trees in the swampy wood were stretching across the pasture. A cold wind from the west made the filly shiver.

"Listen to me, Bill Billings is no Down Easter. Bill Billings is no Boston-bred. I ain't a Johnny Cake, I ain't, and in the matter of breaking horses I reckon I know what

I'm talking about. Madam, do I come into your kitchen and tell you to put more onions in the stew or another pinch of pepper on the beefsteak? Do I show you how to ply your broom or how to lay a fire? No, indeed I do not!"

"I was just seeking information," the housekeeper replied with unusual meekness. It seemed she was getting her way for a change.

"I ain't a Johnny Cake," Billings repeated with a dry chuckle.

"I'm asking because I'm always trying to cut down on expenses," the housekeeper explained. "But I wonder, is it a good plan to buy moldy feed like you just did—even though it's cheaper—when it might make the horses sick?"

"You could be right about Lady Suffolk," the dealer replied. "I have an investment in her, yes, sir. But with those other slugs in there—especially Waterloo—it would make small difference whether they got colic or not."

"Mr. Billings, what's the matter with Waterloo?"

"A white-legged horse is just no good, that's all," he told her. "You've heard the old saw:

> One white leg, inspect him;
> Two white legs, reject him;
> Three white legs, sell him to your foes;
> Four white legs, feed him to the crows!

And you know how many white legs Waterloo has."

"But why did you buy him then?"

The dealer gave his dry chuckle. "Nary a one did he have when I bought him."

"I don't understand."

The light had been red. Now the sun was gone and the

light was green. Lady Suffolk could barely see Stephen in the shadow of the barn. He hadn't moved.

"I ain't a Johnny Cake," the dealer repeated to himself with an air of deep self-satisfaction.

"Mr. Billings," the housekeeper insisted, "why didn't Waterloo have white legs when you bought him?"

"His name was Bonaparte then. I got him at an agricultural fair in New Jersey, from a horse dealer who had come down from Connecticut. Oh, he was smart, that feller, a real Connecticut Yankee—and they're the smartest there is, yes, sir. None smarter. Insisted upon, nay, *demanded*, hard money, he did.

" 'I use paper money to start my fires,' says he. Says he, 'It's hard money or no deal.'

" 'Hard money it is,' says I and paid him two hundred dollars cash money.

"It was a fine spring day, with the sun warm and friendly. But by the time we got off the ferry at Brooklyn, it had started to blow great guns, and before we reached home, a storm had overtaken us. Well, when I had brought Bonaparte into his stall and lit the lantern, I received the shock of my life. What do you expect that was, madam?"

"He had four white legs!"

"Correct! The rain had washed off the dye. That's when he became Waterloo. Oh, that Connecticut Yankee—he was a smart feller, aye, a smart feller!" Billings gave a high-pitched laugh. It sounded like the reedy neigh of an old horse.

"But weren't you mad—I mean angry? Didn't you do something about it?" Mrs. Eller asked, surprised at the man's good humor.

"Oh, I cooked his mutton," the dealer replied.

"How?"

"I'd paid him in counterfeit coin. Hard money he wanted, hard money he got—lead dipped in silver."

"Do tell!" the housekeeper remarked. "But where did you get the counterfeit coins?"

"I had them, madam, I had them. You ask an ocean of questions."

"I hope you didn't use any counterfeit money to buy that filly!" Mrs. Eller exclaimed, as if worried for the dealer's own good.

"Indeed not! Bill Billings is smarter than he might appear. Anyway, this business concerning Waterloo was years ago, when he was a young horse, and when the 'coiners' were considerable active. Well, I've had my money's worth out of him, counterfeit or no. Waterloo's old now and tends to bolt. He ain't worth the powder and shot it would take to feed him to the crows, although he's not through earning his hay and oats yet, no indeed. . . . Look! It's nearly dark!"

"Well, I don't know where the time goes," Mrs. Eller replied, adding, as if she blamed him, "and I haven't even finished fixing supper!"

Twilight had given way to dusk. At the edge of the dark wood, an invisible night bird gave a mournful cry. *"Whippoorwill! Whip, whip, whip, whippoorwill!"*

"Speaking of whips . . ." the dealer remarked, flexing Little Billy, "well, I reckon it's too late now to go on with the lesson."

There was still just enough light to see, and the housekeeper turned away to hide her triumphant smile.

"We'll make up for it tomorrow," Billings said cheerfully. "Dog!" he shouted. "Come get the filly!"

Stephen Seven Trees stepped out from the gloom. He walked to the post, untied the rope, and started to take Lady Suffolk toward the barn. Still terrified from the beating, she balked, snorting.

Stephen slackened the rope. Then, slowly, he walked back to her head. Carefully reaching up, he began to pat her neck. She shifted her feet and continued to snort, but presently she grew quiet.

Stephen then brought her to the trough. Terror and pain had left her bone dry, and she drank deeply. The boy waited patiently until she had finished, then led her back to her stall, bringing hay and oats to the manger.

After that, he disappeared, but she could hear the quick, light sound of his moccasined feet springing up the ladder to the loft, followed by the sound of his footsteps overhead.

She ate in the darkness. Her appetite was considerably less than it had been at noon, and the feed tasted especially bitter. Her spirit had not been broken—it would take many savage beatings before that happened, if it ever did—but her morale was low. She felt confused and abandoned. The welts from the whip lashes had stiffened, sending sharp, hot pains through her whenever she moved. She left most of her supper.

After a while, she heard the sound of steps on the ladder, descending. Something plopped outside her stall, behind her. The footsteps went away, but they soon returned. A swinging lantern made black shadows jump inside the barn. The filly had known lanterns at her former home, but now, in her highly keyed state, she started to neigh and kick the oak walls of her stall.

The yellow light that flickered through the line of wooden pillars was like flames, and fire terrified her. Reacting to the filly, the other horses began to neigh and stamp.

"Hush!" Stephen ordered all of them.

The lantern stopped swinging after he had hung it on a post by the filly's stall. When the shadows no longer jumped and the flamelike flickering quieted to a soft, steady glow, Lady Suffolk began to relax. As she did, so did the other horses.

From the loft, Stephen had brought down a wolf pelt, the legs of which were tied in knots. Untying them, he spread the pelt on the little wooden table where he ate his meals and separated the contents. There was a fine steel hunting knife with a deer-antler handle, several small pottery jars with wooden stoppers, each wrapped in deerskin, a cream-colored square of doeskin upon which a map was drawn in brown ink, a necklace of bear claws, several sea shells, and a wide belt made up of hundreds of tiny, different-colored beads strung on deer thongs. They were all woven together at each end.

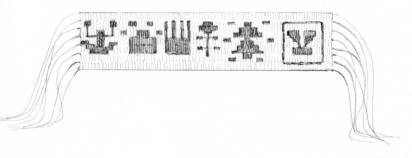

Lady Suffolk heard a soft pop as Stephen removed the stopper from one of the jars. A moment later, she felt a gentle hand on her left hindquarter and moved over to let him pass. The boy walked up to her head and patted her neck, reassuring the filly.

But then a strong, wild odor rose from the jar and filled her nostrils. *Danger*—the message, passed down through thousands upon thousands of her ancestors, going back to prehistoric times, wafted to her from that little pottery jar. She snorted, tossing her head and stamping.

"Hush!" Stephen commanded.

Holding the jar in his right hand, as far from her nose as possible, he kept patting her neck with his left. The stamping died first, then the tossing of the head, and finally the snorts.

The boy edged back sideways until he was standing by her barrel. Gently, he began to pass his free hand over her coat, feeling for the welts. She shied away at first, banging against the opposite wall, but gradually she grew used to his light touch. After that he started to rub the contents of the jar into the welts. Almost at once, they stopped smarting.

"Stephen?" Mrs. Eller called from outside the stall. "Here's your supper. I'm sorry your uncle ate all the chicken, but here are the fixings and a nice apple for you. Hi! What's this?" She held up the doeskin. "A map of where Captain Kidd buried his treasure?"

"No," Stephen answered her.

"What is it then?"

He made no reply.

"What's this with all the beads—wampum?"

"Yes."

"First time I've ever seen this. What do all these figures mean?"

He was silent.

"Stephen, what are you putting on that horse?"

"Bear grease."

"Bear grease! Aren't horses afraid of bears?"

"This is just the grease," he explained.

"This is just the grease!" She mimicked his solemn tone.

"And herbs," he added.

"Where did you get it?"

He did not answer.

"I expect it's some Indian medicine you got from your father," the housekeeper said. "Well, I'm going back to my kitchen. I can get about as much talk out of my broom as you. Now you wash those hands before you eat that supper." She stalked out, muttering, "Bear grease!"

When Stephen had finished treating the welts, he returned the jar to the wolfpelt and put it on the floor. He left out the hunting knife, however. Then he drew a bucket of water at the well and washed his hands with lye soap before sitting down to supper. The "fixings" Mrs. Eller had mentioned were a bowl of boiled potatoes in milk and butter.

Eating with his fingers, the boy finished the last piece of potato, then drank the rich, warm liquid from the bowl. With the hunting knife, he cut the apple into quarters. Entering Lady Suffolk's stall, he offered her a piece, which she readily accepted. They shared the apple, chewing in silence—more or less, enjoying themselves.

4

THE BREAKING IN
OF LADY SUFFOLK

The man who called himself Bill Billings received deep satisfaction from inflicting pain upon other creatures, whether they had two feet or four, but he was not stupid. Good as it made him feel to exercise Little Billy on Lady Suffolk, he managed to hold himself back. He knew full well that, if permanently damaged, she would bring him little or no profit when he sold her—which he planned to do as soon as he had broken her in.

Her training continued the next morning, immediately after Stephen Seven Trees had fed and groomed the horses. She was tied to a post in the barnyard when the dealer approached.

"Good morning, Lady Suffolk," he greeted her in his weak, little voice. "Slept well, I trust. Are we ready for Step Number Two in the Bill Billings System?"

Walking up to the filly's left side, he stood by her head. In his gloved right hand was a leather bridle attached to a bit, which he held in his left hand. He had taken the glove off that hand. The fingers were gnarled and red. On his thumb were two curious scars that stood out a livid white against the red. One was shaped like an H, the other like a T.

Cupping his bare left hand around Lady Suffolk's chin, the dealer slipped his fingers between her lips and into her mouth, where she had no teeth. Disgusted by the taste of his fingers, she curled back her lips, opening her jaws.

"That's right, Lady," Billings whispered.

He jerked the bridle up with his right hand, and the bit slid into her mouth, grating over her front teeth. The mouthpiece was extremely unpleasant—cold, hard, and altogether strange. She tossed her head from side to side, struggling to get rid of the unnatural object. It remained, pinning down her tongue with numbing force. But she went on fighting it.

"Appears to me it's time for Little Billy to have his say," the dealer remarked calmly, as he slipped on his left glove.

The long black whip was never far away. Within seconds, it swished through the air and landed with a *whomp* on the filly's back. Altogether, Little Billy gave her five of his "kisses."

"Now you and your new friend have a nice talk," Billings told Lady Suffolk.

By this time, the bit had warmed in the filly's mouth and no longer felt so foreign. She began to play with it, chomping down on it, moving it about with her tongue and lips. Gradually, almost without her realizing it, the dealer had slipped the bit back until it rested in the corners of her mouth.

Then, with a gentleness surprising in such a man, Billings began to give little pulls on the reins that forced the filly to lower and raise her head, and turn it from side to side. For a while, she struggled against the new tactics, just because they *were* new and therefore strange. She fought the dealer even when he called upon Little Billy once again to help her understand.

Billings did not, however, pull any harder on the reins. At last, Lady Suffolk relaxed her neck and moved her head every way the dealer wanted, which made him chuckle. "I ain't a Johnny Cake, I ain't," he declared—and gave her a few more stripes.

"Dog," he told the boy, who had come up and was quietly standing by, "the way a rider or driver delivers messages to his horse is over 'the leather telegraph'—these reins I have in my hands. You must keep in constant mind that you never—I repeat, *never*—hurt the horse by rough handling of the reins. Beware of Billings if he ever catches you tugging on the reins.

"Of course," he added as an afterthought, "if you *want* to hurt the horse, Little Billy is always ready and willing. But don't ever beat a horse in a stall, Dog, because you'll never be able to get him to go into that stall again. You understand, Dog?"

The boy made no answer.

"A ruined mouth results in a hard pusher, for the horse will begin to push as soon as the driver pulls. A bad-tempered, hasty man," the dealer went on, "will quickly spoil a good-tempered horse."

Stephen remained silent, but he stared up at his uncle with his startling blue eyes, as if unable to believe what he had just heard.

"Do you understand, Dog?" Billings demanded. "I don't know the Montauk word for it, and I wouldn't dirty my mouth using it, if I did. Oh, I see now, you reckon I'm bad-tempered and hasty, do you?"

The boy made no reply. Billings thrust out a gloved hand, clamped his fingers on Stephen's arm, and shook him violently back and forth.

"If you can't talk like a human," he snarled in his whispery voice, "can you *bark*, you stupid Montauk? Can you *growl, pant, whine?*"

There was a long, white blur as the dealer swung his other hand, giving Stephen a cuff on the ear that sent the boy sprawling.

"Why my sister ever married that dirty redskin father of yours, I'll never know," Billings muttered. "Yes, yes, I am aware that he was a Grand Sachem, but for all his power, he's just as dead now as everyone else in his village—and she with him. *She with him!*"

Abruptly he turned away. Over his shoulder he snapped, "Look to the filly."

During the next few months, Lady Suffolk grew to know Little Billy quite well. Little Billy had a long whalebone handle, covered with strips of woven black leather; the lash was of the stoutest whipcord. In the expert hands of the horse dealer, Little Billy's "kisses" were unforgettable. Because he faithfully doctored her welts at the end of each session, Stephen Seven Trees was running out of bear grease.

Contrary to the Bill Billings System as it had been explained to Mrs. Eller by the originator himself, the reward for doing well was not "an apple, carrot, or lump of sugar." From the dealer, the filly received none of these—nor so much as a pat of approval. When she obeyed, the dividend was a short, well-earned rest from Little Billy.

Lady Suffolk's feed, however, began to improve. Now, the hay that Stephen brought to her manger by the forkful was green, sweet smelling, and crisp when she chewed it. The oats were free of dust and mold, although there weren't many of them.

"My principle is to go light on oats until the horse is put to some work," Billings remarked to Stephen during one noon feeding. "A horse that is allowed to reach his full growth normally will be hardier, healthier, and have a more enduring constitution than he would if forced along rapidly by an ocean of oats. Understand, Dog?"

Stephen, as usual, remained silent. But his uncle, caught up in the excitement of expounding on the Bill Billings System, did not notice this at once.

"It will take longer to mature him my way, but he'll last longer. Early maturity is early decay. I'm sure you will agree with me, Dog."

Again the boy made no reply, but once more, Billings passed over the fact.

"They tell us that, in ancient times, the athlete Milo carried a four-year-old heifer through the stadium at Olympia. But it was one he had carried every day since it was a calf. Of course, all that time he had been in training without letup, exhausting his vitality. I expect that Milo died well before the heifer. I repeat, early maturity is early decay. Do you understand me, Dog?"

This time, the dealer noticed Stephen's silence.

"I spoke to you, Dog," he told the boy. "Do I have to bark at you to get an answer? You'd speak quick enough if I threw a bone to you, wouldn't you, you Montauk rascal?"

No matter how they started, the sessions between Stephen and his uncle always seemed to end up the same way —with the swing.

As time passed, Stephen and the filly began to depend on one another more and more, each giving the other strength and spirit, as Billings went on using his gloved hand on the boy and Little Billy on Lady Suffolk. After the bit, the dealer broke the filly to saddle, then to being ridden, and then to the harness.

Although Billings brought her no apples, carrots, or sugar, Stephen had something of this nature for her almost every day. One time, after the night feeding when the boy was sharing his apple with her, he picked up a few of the oats she had left in her manger and popped them into his mouth. He chewed them gamely and finally swallowed them, but he didn't like them much. Another time, he took the hat he was wearing and put it on her head. Her ears got in the way, and, finally, their twitching knocked the hat off, but it was fun.

She was in the pasture one cold morning when he came out, carrying a wooden bucket, and he whistled to her. "Whit-too-wheet!"

She frisked away. He took the bucket, rattling the contents, and put it down. Then he walked off. She trotted up to the bucket and sniffed inside. Oats! She took a mouthful and was chewing it when the boy started to walk toward her. She shied away. He picked up the bucket and started for the barn. She followed him at a distance. When he put the bucket down again and walked off, she once more trotted up and began to eat the oats. He came back for the bucket a second time, and she shied away again, but, the next time, she held her ground when he returned. He stood by her shoulder, patting her silently as she finished off the oats.

By the third day, when the "Whit-too-wheet!" sounded in the pasture, she came running to him, and not just for the snack he offered. She danced around him, tossing her head up and down. She trotted forward and lay her head over his shoulder, rubbing her silky cheek against his. She whinnied long and repeatedly.

That night, she was just dropping off to sleep when she heard a voice saying softly, "Lady Suffolk!"

She felt a light tap on her hindquarters and moved over. Stephen walked up to her head and patted her, then took her from her stall, through the dark barn, and out into the crisp, moonlit night. Leading her to a tree stump in the barnyard, he halted her, then stepped onto the stump and sprang lightly onto her back.

He sat just behind her withers, perfectly balanced. She felt his knees and heels on her barrel. The boy and the filly were both completely at ease, fully confident in each other. With no word or sign from him, she started forward at a walk, then began to trot. She went faster and faster until she broke into a canter, then a hard, rolling gallop.

Feeling her muscles moving between his thighs, Stephen leaned forward. Around the pasture they went, less a boy and a horse than a "boy-horse," a single unit. When she

leaned inward on the curves, he leaned with her. He heard and felt her drumming hoofs as if they were his own.

The cold night came rushing into their faces, and the round, pale moon sped through the stormy sky, keeping pace with them, bathing everything in their path with a soft bluish light. When they finally drew up, both their chests were heaving, pumping great clouds of silvery vapor from their nostrils into the darkness. Their hearts were pounding, and their warm blood was rushing through their bodies.

That night, they both slept well.

5

A SET OF SHOES

Each day, the sun came up later than before and set earlier. Every morning, frost covered the ground, sparkling in the pale sunlight. Stephen Seven Trees began his days chopping up the layer of ice in the trough so he could water the horses. He always warmed the bits before putting them into their mouths. He had just finished grooming the horses one blustery December morning when his uncle entered the barn.

"Hitch the filly and Waterloo to the wagon," he ordered. "We're going to the blacksmith's."

In their traces, the two horses waited quietly for the dealer. Although the day was just starting, Waterloo appeared tired. He was quite an old horse. His lower lip hung loose. His knees seemed on the verge of buckling and made a clicking noise whenever he shifted his weight. His temples were sunken, and his withers jutted up like a pair of ax blades in his loose hide.

He moved out smartly, however, when Billings climbed

aboard the wagon and brought Little Billy into play. Stephen trotted along behind the wagon. His uncle kept up the brisk pace, so that, although the journey was rather long, it took them less than a half hour. Both horses and Stephen were blowing when the dealer drew up at the blacksmith's. Billings unhitched Lady Suffolk and brought her into the shop.

Facing them was an enormous brick fireplace, through one side of which stuck the nozzle of a mighty bellows. The wooden floor was burned in a thousand places by sparks and the U-shaped imprint of hot horseshoes. From the low rafters, clamps and hammers and other tools hung by the scores, like sleeping bats.

The blacksmith was a wiry, bandy-legged man, in a greasy leather apron. He had a round, bald head that was set like a stone on his short, grimy neck, and his rolled-up sleeves revealed arms knotted with muscle. His son, a thickset boy with small, mean-looking eyes and curly orange hair, stood by the bellows.

"I want the filly shod," Billings told the smith.

"Let me see her way of going," the other man said.

"Dog," the dealer ordered.

Stephen led Lady Suffolk out again and vaulted upon her back, riding her up and down the road as the others watched.

"He rides well," the smith remarked to no one in particular as the horse and rider returned.

Stephen dropped his eyes shyly. The smith's son sniffed in contempt.

"You see, Jimmy," the smith told his son, "her action is low and of a daisy-cutting character. She steals along like a fox, with her head straight out. You notice how she brings her left rear hoof up higher than the others? We'll fix that —make that shoe a mite heavier."

They brought the filly back into the shop, and Jimmy began to pump the bellows. The pile of red coals in the forge flared and blue flames flickered up. Lady Suffolk snorted nervously.

"Don't be afraid," the smith told her. Squatting down, he picked up one hoof after the other, studying each thoroughly. Straightening up, he commented, "I've seen bigger."

Carefully, he selected four horseshoes from a pile by the forge. With a pair of tongs, he thrust them one by one into the heart of the glowing coals. When they were red-hot, he took one out and began to bang it on his anvil, the red sparks flying. His son was watching him intently.

"The good blacksmith, Jimmy," the man said, "fits the shoe to the horse's hoof—he does *not* trim the hoof to fit the shoe."

The smith held the hot iron against the filly's hoof. There was a hissing and a cloud of smoke rose, but she felt no pain. The smith returned the shoe to the coals and hammered another few hundred sparks out of it before he was satisfied. Again, there was a loud hiss and a cloud of vapor as he plunged the shoe into a bucket of water. Then he held the iron against Lady Suffolk's hoof and began to nail it on. He was driving the nails right into her hoof.

They did not hurt, however, and she stood on three legs until he had finished the job. He repeated the process on her other hoofs.

[55]

When Billings had paid, the smith's son drew his father to one side and whispered in his ear.

"My boy says he can out-wrestle yours," the smith reported.

"He's not my boy," Billings answered, "but your son can try conclusions with him, if he has a mind to."

They all walked out into the front yard, the dealer leading Lady Suffolk by her bridle.

The two boys began to circle, hands out, ready to clutch. They were about the same height, but Jimmy was at least twenty pounds heavier. They were like a terrier and a bulldog. Stephen watched his opponent warily. He had never really caught his breath from the long run to the blacksmith's and now he was breathing deeply.

"It's the Yankee way," the smith remarked with a nod of his bald head and a knowing wink. "Life is competition, fightin' an' gittin'. The sooner they learn it, the better, by crackey. Go it, Jimmy!"

The dealer watched in silence. Lady Suffolk whinnied nervously, and Billings tightened his hold on her bridle.

Jimmy gave a contemptuous sniff. Then he lunged forward, seized Stephen with both hands on the upper arms, and flung him back and forth, trying to hurl him to the ground. Though Stephen's legs flew about, he landed on his feet each time.

Jimmy thrust out his hip and tried to yank Stephen over it, but the smaller boy twisted away. The blacksmith's son got a headlock on him, choking him. With a quick jerk, Stephen broke the hold. Both boys were breathing heavily now. Although Stephen was not nearly as strong as his adversary, he was much quicker. The trouble was that he couldn't make his tired muscles move as fast as he wanted them to.

Lady Suffolk stamped about, neighing. The dealer held her bridle with both hands, watching the fight in fascination. Grunting, squirming, bodies slippery with sweat in spite of the cold, arms and legs entangled like vines, the two boys tottered around the yard, wobbling like a top that is coming to the end of its spin. Then they fell heavily to the earth, so heavily that Lady Suffolk felt the ground shake under her.

The blacksmith gave a cry of disbelief and dismay. The half-blood was on top of his boy, pinning him down!

The fall had knocked the wind out of Jimmy and he lay on his back, desperately trying to get his lungs working. His mean little eyes glared up at Stephen, who met the hot gaze calmly for ten seconds or more, then released the other's arms and started to crawl off him. Lady Suffolk gave a joyous neigh.

Doubling his fist, Jimmy swung his arm, twisting his torso and digging his heel into the ground, so that the punch had all his weight behind it. The blow hit Stephen full in the mouth. He fell back dazed, and, at once, Jimmy was on him, pumping fists, elbows, and knees into his unprotected body.

"Rough and tumble!" the blacksmith yelled. "Go it, Jimmy!"

Stephen managed to clear his battered brain and, rolling away, scrambled to his feet. Jimmy lowered his head and charged, intending to butt the other boy in the stomach. Stephen leaped aside and his opponent rushed past like a bull, sprawling in the dirt when Stephen shoved him.

[57]

But the smaller boy's legs were losing their spring, and the next time his adversary charged, he could not dodge quickly enough.

Jimmy's big, hard head, with the weight of his entire body behind it, slammed into Stephen's stomach. The "wrestling" match was over, although Jimmy managed to get in several more good blows before his father pulled him off.

"Shake hands now," the smith ordered the boys. "No grudges. It's the Yankee way."

Stephen could barely see the other boy through his rapidly closing eyelids, but he did notice the smirk on Jimmy's dirty, sweat-streaked face.

"I expect you'd best ride in the wagon, Dog," Billings told him. "You've about had your fill of exercise today, I reckon."

He and the smith bid each other a cordial good-day. The fight seemed to have satisfied the dealer in some way, and he did not work Little Billy as much as he could have on the ride home. Her new iron shoes felt heavy and awkward on Lady Suffolk's hoofs, but she soon grew used to them and they were good protection against the rocks and stones in the road.

Stephen lay silently on the hard boards in the back of the wagon, like a package of meat, rolling about in the rough, rumbling drive. That evening, he stood for a long, long time in the stall with Lady Suffolk, his arms around her strong, warm neck. And late that night they had another gallop in the moonlight.

6

FOUR WHITE LEGS

Now that Lady Suffolk was shod, unless the weather was particularly foul, Billings regularly took her out on the road, hitched to the wagon with Waterloo.

They jogged six or more miles a day, through the misty, gray Long Island winter, with lively spurts now and then of a quarter mile or so that made the filly's chest heave and sent the vapor jetting from her nostrils, as though from the spout of a boiling tea kettle.

"Any party that claims he can lay down fixed rules for working a horse is either a fool or an imposter—and most likely both," the dealer remarked to Stephen in one of his expansive moods, one chill morning. "Everyone must go to the devil by his own road, but, to have good horseflesh, you must put the right distance into it. If your horse is dead beat after only a few miles, your horse is of small value."

Waterloo was a good horse to work with, in spite of his age and nervousness. Trotting along beside him, Lady Suffolk learned to place her hoofs as he did. They swung their left forelegs and right hindlegs forward together, then their right forelegs and left hindlegs, so that they were like a pair of frigates sailing along on an even keel, with a fine stern wind.

For all their neat precision, however, Lady Suffolk and Waterloo were no match for the relentless stagecoach. As soon as the *Er-r-r-rah, er-r-r-rah!* of the driver's horn sounded behind her, the filly knew she must expect attention from Little Billy. The blaring horn sounded the start of still another wild, hopeless race that always left her and the bay completely blown, cruelly whipped, and badly beaten.

Without fail, the swaying egg-shaped coach thundered past, the haughty driver blind to the other vehicle that was pelted with a barrage of mud and pebbles, thrown up by his horses' drumming hoofs and the stage's rumbling wheels.

As the weather grew steadily worse, Waterloo and Lady Suffolk slipped and slid on the ice and frozen roads, wrenching their muscles and ligaments. Stephen kept busy applying liniments, which brought the blood flowing to the injured spot and gave relief. But when he groomed the filly at the end of an arduous, disheartening day, the brush in his firm, gentle hands was like a caress that did more for her than a gallon of medication.

One particularly foul January afternoon, Billings left the wagon outside a tavern and went in to warm himself by the fire and have a glass or two. The day had begun badly, with still another doomed race with a stagecoach. It worsened. A walloping wind came out of the south, bringing thick swirls of gray sea mist, along with torrents of rain and rattling, stinging sleet. The afternoon was so wet and windy and wild that it seemed as if the whole of Long Island, like a ponderous barge, had broken loose from its moorings and gone wobbling out into the boisterous Atlantic.

The two horses stood, taking the onslaught of the weather quietly. Only their eyes, ears and nostrils moved when water ran in. The bay was still tired and out of sorts from the painful race with the stagecoach. Otherwise, what happened then would never have happened.

A tiny yellow mongrel, a dog no bigger than a cat—and with half a cat's fierce pride—came shambling along the wet road toward the pair on a long, lonely journey from nowhere to nowhere. Tail between his legs, head down, ears laid back, he was a nameless cur that was thoroughly beaten down—not by just this day but by all the miserable days before it, with their swung sticks and thrown stones and marrowless, meatless bones.

Yet, at the sight and smell of the two horses, he paused and seemed to gather himself together. Here were two animals tremendously larger than he was, and at least as cold and wet and wretched as he. Head, ears, and tail shot up together, and he charged the horses, barking his defiance. That was when Waterloo bolted.

He raced down the winding road, and Lady Suffolk had to go along with him, the empty wagon bouncing and banging around behind them. They splashed through deep puddles, their hoofs throwing cold water and mud by the bucketful against their bellies. The bay, wild-eyed and mad with terror, was galloping, but the filly kept up with him in a trot, her legs moving like pistons.

When Waterloo finally drew up, they were both blown,

and the vapor from their wet, overheated bodies smoked up into the cold air. The bay stood with his head down, breathing noisily, knees clicking.

Two boys came running up. Clambering into the wagon, they turned the horses around and started back up the road. "Did you see that little gray horse?" one asked his companion. "She kept up with the bay and never broke her trot!"

"And they were traveling, too," the other replied.

The two boys weren't the only ones who had witnessed the event. Billings and several other men were standing outside the tavern in the rain when the horses came jogging up. (The little yellow dog had continued his endless journey in the best of spirits.)

"Him in a gallop and her trotting right along with him," one of the men said wonderingly. "I've never seen anything like it."

"That's a mighty nice little filly of yours," a burly man in a floppy hat told Billings. "If she was only big enough to stand hard work, you might expect a good deal from her."

"She's big enough to stand hard work, sir," the dealer replied. "And, sir, I *do* expect a good deal from her. The other one, of course, isn't worth the powder and shot it would take to send him to the devil. . . . Here, lads!" he called, tossing a couple of coins to the two boys. "A small reward for your labors."

The boys caught the coppers, looked down at them in their palms, then exchanged rueful glances. The reward was indeed small. Leaving Lady Suffolk and Waterloo out in the storm, the group of men returned to the tavern to celebrate the spectacle of one horse trotting while another galloped.

Billings was in no hurry to leave the cozy spot. By the time they finally returned to their home barn, both horses were thoroughly soaked, chilled, and exhausted. The dealer left them in the care of Stephen Seven Trees and, wobbling more than usual, limped across the drowned yard to the farmhouse, yelling for Mrs. Eller and supper.

Stephen worked long and hard over the horses, and when he finished the hour was late. By then, the storm had blown itself out, and the only sound was the drip of water from the eaves. The moon shone down from a clear, purple sky, but there was no moonlight trot for Lady Suffolk and Stephen that night.

Next morning, the filly was awakened by a frantic scratching of hoofs and screams of terror and pain from the next stall. Waterloo was down, paralyzed in the hindquarters. He kept struggling with his forelegs, his head high, eyes bugging with bewilderment and fear.

The dealer rushed into the barn, his tall, thin form wobbling back and forth like a metronome. His hair and beard were snarled and his eyes were inflamed. He had jumped out of bed, pulling on trousers and boots. He held a blanket around his naked torso. He was wearing his white gloves.

Gazing down at Waterloo, he recited slowly and rather sadly, for him:

> One white leg, inspect him;
> Two white legs, reject him;
> Three white legs, sell him to your foes;
> Four white legs, feed him to the crows. . . .

[65]

The bay made a desperate effort to get to his feet. It failed. At times, he bent his neck to look around at his haunches with his big, perplexed eyes as if trying to see why there was no more power in those thighs that had driven him so many years.

"Easy, Waterloo," Billings told him. "Easy."

The blanket fell away from the dealer's shoulders. For a second or two, before he snatched it up and wrapped it around him, his back was exposed. The skin was reddish, like the rest of him, but it had a complex series of scars— long, ugly white marks like stripes, that sometimes were entangled with each other.

A scuffling sounded as Stephen Seven Trees climbed down the ladder from the loft. Billings glanced over his shoulder, then pulled the blanket tighter around him. The boy stumbled, yawning, still half-asleep. He stared at the stricken bay with widening eyes.

"Well, Dog, I hope we haven't disturbed your slumbers," his uncle remarked dryly. "But you're just in time to bid Waterloo good-by."

Then Billings turned and limped out of the barn. Stephen reached in and patted Lady Suffolk, then filled a bucket from the trough and let the bay drink. Waterloo was very thirsty. He made a final attempt to get to his feet, but, like the others, this was a dismal failure. He bent his neck to stare for the last time at the hindquarters that had suddenly betrayed him after such long, faithful service. At this point, Billings returned.

"Go get your breakfast, Dog," he ordered.

Stephen made no move to go. Obviously, he wanted to stay with Waterloo and help him in any way he could.

"I said go get your breakfast!" his uncle repeated, cuffing Stephen with his gloved left hand. The boy staggered out of the barn. Billings stood, waiting motionless for a while.

Lady Suffolk snorted nervously and pawed the straw of her stall. She sensed, could almost smell, the menace looming in the barn.

From under the blanket, holding it with his gloved right hand, the dealer drew a long, dark, vicious-looking object that gave off a metallic gleam in the early morning light.

"Four white legs, feed him to the crows," he murmured.

Waterloo lay on his side, exhausted, his great whip-marked chest expanding and contracting as he struggled for air. Wild with pain and terror, his large, bloodshot eye stared up at Billings.

In the confines of the four walls, the explosion was deafening. Amid the humming quiet that followed, the sharp, ominous fumes of burnt gunpowder drifted through the raw morning air of the barn like an evil spirit seeking escape. But Waterloo lay still at last, released from further torment by the leaden present from the dark riddle of a man who now gazed down at his lifeless form with rare sympathy.

7

"CALL ME HORSE"

Spring! The heart that had beat so slowly during the long, dark retreat of winter began to throb with an impatient, compelling vigor as light and warmth flooded back to the earth. Timid before, the sun now became steadily bolder, rising earlier and setting later each day—a blazing sphere that sent keen rays down between the long, speeding clouds of March and April.

Bright green grass, popping out with dandelions and clover, spread across the pasture. The sap was rising, the buds were sprouting. The forest was loud with the military tattoo of the woodpecker by day and the steady ringing of the cricket by night. Day and night, the quiet chuckle of the water in creeks and streams sounded as they pushed around and over the pebbles and boulders, flashing in the sunlight, glowing in the moonlight, making haste to the distant sea. Spring was a happy season.

As busy as Billings arranged to keep both of them, Lady Suffolk and Stephen Seven Trees were able to spend some free time together in the pasture almost every day. When she heard the boy's whistled "Whit-too-wheet!" she came running. She frisked about him, dancing, laying her nose playfully over his shoulder, and giving long, slow whinnies. Without much success, Stephen tried to imitate the neighing cry. With more success, he copied her trot, thrusting his left foot and right arm forward together, then his right foot and left arm. Sometimes, when the mood struck him, he got down on his hands and knees in the pasture and grazed with her. Almost every night now, they went for a trot in the moonlight or starshine.

Stephen seldom talked to her directly, but he had two songs that he chanted softly, his lips close to her ear. One was:

> Lady Suffolk came out of her lodge
> And sniffed the morning breeze.
> White dew lay on the grass,
> And the trees sang the song of spring,
> The sweet song of spring,
> The sweet, soft, sighing song of spring. . . .

The other he usually chanted when he was grooming her at the end of the day:

> She's a mighty gray horse
> Oh, she is, yes she is,
> She's a mighty gray horse
> That can sleep standing up,
> And can trot all day long!

So close had the boy and horse become that Stephen could actually feel the impact of Little Billy on her, just as she reacted to Billing's open gloved hand striking the boy. When the dealer beat her or Stephen, she cried out, but the boy endured both the hand on him and the whip on her in silence.

Stephen was chanting his grooming song to Lady Suffolk one afternoon when she suddenly stiffened. Through her, the boy knew that his uncle had entered the barn.

"Dog, don't be all day with that filly," Billings snapped. "You've got other chores to do to earn your keep, you know."

Slowly, Stephen turned and faced his uncle in a way he never had before. Speaking in a quiet but clear voice, he said, "If you have to call me an animal, call me 'Horse.' "

"You can talk!" the dealer exclaimed.

"Of course I can talk," Stephen replied coldly. "You've heard me before."

"Only 'My name is Stephen Seven Trees,' " his uncle retorted, mocking the boy's solemn manner.

"Well, that *is* my name," Stephen pointed out.

"That's next kin to nonsense," Billings snarled. "Your name *was* Stephen Seven Trees when you were living in that filthy Montauk village. But that was two years ago, and the village is no more—everyone dead and the huts burnt to the ground. Now you're living in white man's country and your name is what I say it is, which is Dog. So now then, Dog, what is your name?"

"Stephen Seven Trees," the boy replied.

The impact of an open white hand staggered him. The boy took the blow silently, as usual, but Lady Suffolk began to stamp in her stall, neighing long and loud.

"What's your name?"

"Stephen Seven Trees."

The dealer hit the boy again.

"What's your name?"

Since his mouth was beginning to puff, it was difficult for Stephen to talk, but he answered carefully, "Stephen Seven Trees." It was a croak. Anyhow, it was drowned out by the racket Lady Suffolk was creating. She had never made more noise in her life.

"Mr. Billings, what's the hubbub?" the housekeeper demanded. She stood in the barn door, gripping a broom. "What are you doing to that little horse?"

"I am doing nothing to 'that little horse,' madam, as you can see," the dealer replied dryly. "I wish you would free your mind of 'that little horse.' The *doing* entirely concerns a dirty Montauk rascal who's so completely, utterly stupid he doesn't know his own name."

"Lo! Look at his face! You're fixing to kill him!"

Charging forward, Mrs. Eller swung the broom like a butted musket, slamming it against the side of the dealer's head, staggering him as he had his nephew. She swung again, from the other side, sending him on an extended stagger that way. Then she raised the broom and, with all her might, which was considerable, brought it down with a *thwack* on the top of her employer's head. He grunted, let go of Stephen, and grabbed onto a post to keep from falling.

"I have never struck a woman," the dealer remarked fuzzily, as if indicating that he was about to alter his life-long course of action.

"Strike this one and see what happens," Mrs. Eller suggested. She stood, feet wide apart, her big, red hands grasping the handle of the revolving broom.

Billings started to reply, then shrugged his narrow shoulders and limped out of the barn.

"Stephen, I'll get you your supper—if you can eat it," the housekeeper said in a softer tone. "First, wash the blood off your face. After you eat, if you have any of that magic bear grease left, I expect you might find a use for it."

When she carried the boy's supper into the barn a few minutes later, he had washed his face and brought down the wolf pelt from the loft. He drank the bowlful of buttermilk and managed to eat some bread and cheese, but had to leave the rest.

Mrs. Eller did not return at once to the kitchen with the plates, as she usually did. Instead, she stood, gazing down at the boy, with her muscular arms folded across her wide, spare chest.

"Lucky thing for you the filly made such a hubbub," she remarked, "or I'd never have known you were learning the Bill Billings System."

"I'm glad you came," Stephen told her.

"And I!" the housekeeper agreed, hugging herself. With those arms, the embrace had to hurt a bit. "I haven't felt this good in years," she went on. "I do believe, though, that if I could have given him just one more lick, he would have gone down. . . . Ah, well, another time. Let's see about that face of yours."

"I can do it," the boy said.

"I know you can, Stephen, but I can do it better," she replied firmly. "Get your bear grease."

He untied the wolf pelt, took out a jar, and removed the stopper. The gray grease was in the very bottom of the jar.

He opened another jar. It was filled to the brim with a black substance.

"Lo! What's that?" Mrs. Eller exclaimed.

Stephen popped the stopper back in place. "Paint."

"War paint?" she asked.

"No, Mrs. Eller, not war paint." He opened a third jar, and the strong, wild smell of the bear grease arose from it.

"What kind of paint then?" the housekeeper asked.

"Just paint, Mrs. Eller," the boy replied coldly.

Annoyed at his tone, the housekeeper snapped, "You know something, Stephen? It's not that you don't talk much—it's that you don't say anything when you *do* talk. You are forever trying to make a secret of things. It appears to me that you are a little exalted in the head on that subject. I'm not trying to pry into your personal life. I admit I have a normal woman's curiosity, but I don't think I'm nosy, do you?"

The boy was silent, playing with the beads of the wampum belt. Lady Suffolk snorted nervously.

"Do you, Stephen?" Mrs. Eller demanded. She leaned down toward him like a bird pecking.

"No." He did not look up.

"Stephen, I'm your *friend*."

He looked up. "I know."

"And I reckon I just proved it to Mr. Billing's satisfaction, at least," she went on.

"You did."

"Well, then." She straightened up.

Stephen drew a deep breath. "Mrs. Eller, we use the black paint in our religion—"

She threw up her big, red hands. "Never you mind! I

don't care to hear about that now, I really don't, and that's the truth." She crouched down to examine the wampum on the wolf pelt. "It must have taken months to shape all those beads."

"We call them 'pony beads,' " Stephen told her.

"Do tell," she said. "Pony beads."

"They're made out of clam shells," he went on. "The purple beads are worth twice as much as the white ones. They're all strung on deer sinew."

"Do tell!"

"The men gathered the shells during the summer and stored them in great piles," Stephen told her. "Then the women made them into wampum during the winter. Wampum was like a charm to the Indians on Long Island, my father said. To us, it had more value than gold or silver."

"Do tell!" she repeated, meaning exactly that.

"Every tribe had its Wampum Keeper. The tribes exchanged wampum like gifts, to show that there was friendship between the two. A runner who came before a council without a wampum belt would get no attention. Black wampum meant war, death, or sorrow. White wampum meant purity, faith, or peace."

"But listen now," the housekeeper broke in. "What if one tribe got mad at another—I mean angry—and wanted to go on the warpath after the two tribes had exchanged white belts?"

"Then that tribe would send the other one its wampum painted black or soaked in blood."

"Soaked in blood!"

"Captives were ransomed with wampum," Stephen continued, the words pouring from his lips like spring water gushing through a creek after the long lockup of winter. "And usually, when a treaty or some agreement was made, two belts of the same kind were woven, and each party kept one."

"This wampum is mainly white beads," she remarked. "I expect it's some kind of treaty or agreement."

Stephen did not reply.

"A body could almost make out the figures. *That* looks like a tree, and *that* looks like a flower—they *are* figures, aren't they, Stephen?"

"Yes."

"Do you know what they mean?"

The boy was silent. Once again sensing the tension in the barn, Lady Suffolk shifted her weight, banging her barrel against the boards of her stall.

"Do you know what they mean, Stephen?"

Quietly, the boy answered at last, "Yes, Mrs. Eller. I know what they mean."

8

THE BLACK FACE

The housekeeper chuckled. "Pay me no mind, Stephen. I don't mean to pry. . . . Well, this isn't getting your face back into fix."

Opening another jar, filled with bear grease, she wrinkled her nose at the smell. As big and rough as her hands were, Mrs. Eller's touch was surprisingly gentle. Slowly, carefully, almost daintily, her thick red fingers worked the gray salve over the cuts and bruises of the boy's face.

"You shouldn't hate your uncle, Stephen," she remarked.

"Huh!"

"I know how he has treated you, but he *is* your mother's brother."

"And *I*'m my mother's son."

"I know, I know. He does seem to forget that, doesn't he?"

"He hates Indians, and I'm my *father*'s son."

"I expect he *does* hate Indians, but he hates everybody and everything—especially stagecoaches."

"And horses," the boy added. "When he isn't knocking 'the Montauk rascal' around, he's exercising Little Billy on the horses."

She drew back to check the results of her work and to study his face. "But, listen now, Stephen," she said. "He showed a different side of himself that time when Waterloo was out of fix."

The boy snorted. "He wouldn't even let me stay and take care of Waterloo."

Mrs. Eller's voice was suddenly soft. "That is exactly what I mean, Stephen. He didn't want you to be there when he shot him."

"Why did he have to shoot him?"

"It was an act of mercy, Stephen. The horse was paralyzed. Your uncle put him out of his misery."

"He put him *through* enough misery in his life."

"I know. I would not call Mr. Billings a kindhearted man. But I do believe there is some good in him—there *has* to be—he's your mother's brother, and I've heard what a fine person she was."

"From who? My uncle?"

"No, Stephen, not from your uncle. He's hardly ever mentioned her to me. I expect it's too painful for him. She's probably the only person he's ever loved."

"Who told you about her, then?"

"Stephen, it's a well-known fact, in this part of the Island at least, that when the smallpox broke out in your father's village and she brought you here, she could have stayed here, too. She had nothing to gain by going back—your father was already dead. But she returned to take care of the sick, even though she knew it was almost certain death for her, which it was."

The boy was quiet. Sensing his sadness, Lady Suffolk neighed to him softly.

"I expect your mother's death made your uncle even worse—he was never cruel to you till after she died, if you remember—but his heart was already hardened to the world. Something happened to him when he was out in Tennessee on one of those trips, I'm sure of it. It has to do with stagecoaches and his limp and those famous gloves of his. Have you ever seen him without them?"

"Not I."

"Nor *I*. Do you know he never takes them off, even when he's eating—or sleeping? He must have twenty pair in his dresser, all silk. Those gloves just *have* to be covering up something. Maybe his hands were burned in a fire, or maybe he had a finger or two bitten off in a fight—I've seen worse happen on the frontier, you can believe me."

"You mean he stuffs cotton or something in his gloves, to fill up the empty fingers?" Stephen asked.

"Maybe, I'm saying. Or maybe he was in a stagecoach wreck, and broke his leg and smashed his hands at the same time. He *does* hate those stages, although I expect it's partly because they go faster than he can. Whether it's dealing in horseflesh or racing it, Mr. Billings has the strongest desire to come out on top."

Mrs. Eller had finished doctoring Stephen's face by now. He reached into Lady Suffolk's stall and patted her, remarking, "I'd like to take her out West."

The housekeeper's face stiffened with alarm. "Don't," she told him earnestly. "Don't *ever*!"

"You mean they'd kill me because I'm a dirty redskin?" the boy asked coldly.

"Of course I don't mean that, Stephen. I'm surprised you would even think that of me. Listen now, I *know* the frontier—at least the way it was twenty-five years ago, and it couldn't have improved much since then. You've seen yon forest and how dismal and dreary it is. Well, imagine that forest stretching for hundreds and hundreds of miles, with just a log cabin in a little clearing once in a great while— a falling-down cabin, with broken windows patched with old coats and hats. That's what it's like in the West—one huge, dark, gloomy forest, filled with bears and wolves and screaming painters—"

"What are 'screaming painters'?" Stephen asked.

"What they call panthers."

"All that sounds exciting to me," he replied.

"Of course it would to a boy like you, Stephen, but you don't understand. It's not only the wild animals. The worst danger in the forest by far is the people. They'd kill you, not because you're half-Indian but just because you're alive. The forest changes people, Stephen."

"How?" he asked.

"The way it changed your uncle. It makes people wilder, and crueler, and careless of others' lives. Life is held very cheap on the frontier. My husband's life was worth two quarters of a dollar. That's the amount of money he was carrying when two land pirates tomahawked him as he was coming home on the Natchez Trace—two quarters of a dollar!"

"They killed him?" Stephen asked, shocked.

"They killed him," she replied, adding grimly, "but

they didn't get far before the Regulators caught them. Hanged the two on the spot, the Regulators did, then cut their heads off with a butcher knife and stuck them on poles along the Trace."

"What are 'Regulators'?"

"Private citizens who band together 'to preserve law and order,' as they say. The Regulators insisted that I come see their work. They were right proud of themselves, they were, and acted like they expected me to be pleased. They buried the rest of the two land pirates at a crossroads, like a couple of werewolves, so that all the horses and wagons would pass over the grave."

"Werewolves!" Stephen exclaimed.

"They didn't bury them deep enough, though, and after the first good rain, the bodies appeared," she went on, her face tight and pale. "Headless, bones broken by the wagon wheels, the splintered ends sticking up out of the mud, they made a horrible sight. . . . That, Stephen, is when the young widow of James W. Eller decided she had had enough of the frontier and returned to civilization."

"I'm very sorry, Mrs. Eller," the boy told her. Then he added, "But the Regulators must have caught and hanged most of the land pirates by now."

"Hang two and two more appear, popping up like toadstools," she replied. "That's what the forest does to men. The Regulators, themselves, are bad enough. Their idea of rare sport is to catch a wolf, cut the tendons on its hind legs so it can't run, then turn their dogs loose on it. That's 'rare sport,' Stephen. They have the same kind of fun with the bear cubs they catch. But nobody sings louder than the Regulators when the circuit rider makes his rounds."

"What's a 'circuit rider'?"

"The preacher who travels from one community to the other, holding church services." She shook her head in sad discouragement. "Stephen, Stephen, Stephen, I fear I'm not making you see the frontier as it is—the gloom, the mind-killing dullness, the *horror*."

"I think I understand."

"The fights I've seen! Men clawing and biting each other like wild animals—anything's fair—'rough and tumble,' they call it."

"I know," the boy replied dryly. " 'The Yankee way.' "

"There was a man called Bear Claw, on the Trace," she continued.

Stephen asked warily, "An Indian?"

"A white man. He had a piece of iron shaped like a bear's claw that he'd strap onto his hand in a fight. You can imagine what that would do to another man's face. . . . Bear claw," she repeated, thoughtfully. "Let's see that wampum again!"

Coming around to Stephen's side of the wolf pelt, she gazed down at the band of beads. "Yes, I thought that looked familiar somehow," she remarked, pointing to a figure. "That's a bear claw!"

"And what's this next to it?" Stephen asked.

"Why, it looks like the paw print of a dog!" she exclaimed.

He asked softly, "Or a wolf?"

"A wolf, yes!"

"That was my father's name: Wolf Bear," Stephen explained proudly. "The Montauks, and all the other tribes, I reckon, have no written language. All our religion and history and legends are passed down from father to son. Important people in the tribe have names that can be shown in a picture or in wampum."

The housekeeper pointed to another form in the belt. "This thing that looks like a tree," she said. "Is that you?"

"Yes. Montauks are sometimes given place names. Where I was born, there were seven pine trees around our wigwam."

"But there's only one here," she pointed out.

"It would be too much trouble to weave seven different trees," he told her. "You see those purple beads around the tree?"

She counted them aloud. "There are only six. Where's the seventh?"

He pointed to the figure of the tree, itself, saying, "I'm only a stupid Montauk rascal, but even *I* could figure that out."

She chuckled. "How clever! Stephen," she added, after a pause, do you realized we've talked more in the last few minutes than we've done in two whole years?"

"Yes, but what about my uncle?"

"I am not concerned about your uncle," the housekeeper replied. "I am fully confident that he will keep to his bed for a while yet, as the result of that last swat I fetched him. Stephen, what's this figure that looks like a flower?"

"That's my mother."

"What was her name?"

"Before she married my father, it was Kate Harnett," he answered.

"You mean Kate *Billings*," the housekeeper corrected him.

"No, Harnett," Stephen said, puzzled.

"Do tell!"

"I remember I saw her name one time in her family Bible, along with the name of her brother William. I hadn't thought about that till now. What does it mean?"

"Well, I don't know," she replied. "Maybe Mr. Billings is not your real uncle. Or maybe he's known in the West by the name of William Harnett, when he'd rather not be."

"I expect we'd learn something if we could unpeel those gloves," Stephen suggested.

"I wouldn't care to risk it now," she told him. "Mr. Billings is a mighty light sleeper, even when he's had a knock or two, and I'd rather jump into a pit with a pair of wildcats than try conclusions with him when he's truly aroused. Stephen, how can this figure represent your mother when it looks like a flower?"

"When she married my father, she took a Montauk name—Heather Blossom," he explained. "You see, this wampum is a message that says that Wolf Bear and Heather Blossom—"

"What's wrong?" the housekeeper asked in dismay. "Stephen, what in the world is the matter?"

The boy had stopped short, eyes wide and staring, mouth open. Blood draining from his face left the skin a sickly yellow. Lady Suffolk shifted her weight, stamping nervously.

"What *is* it, Stephen?"

When at last he spoke, his voice was small and dry. "The names of the dead should never be spoken. It's bad luck."

Mrs. Eller reached out a big, red hand toward the boy,

gazing down at him with deep concern. She opened her mouth to tell him that he shouldn't be afraid of a silly Indian superstition, especially when he was only half Montauk.

No words came out. She kept silent, holding back just short of touching him. To her it was a silly superstition. To him it was a religious belief.

"I'm sorry, Stephen," the housekeeper said. "I am truly sorry. I didn't mean to pry. . . ."

But not another word or sign of life could she get out of him. At last, she picked up the dishes and carried them into the house. He continued to sit, staring straight ahead, as mute as in the old days when the horse dealer had first started to call him Dog.

"Lady Suffolk!" a familiar voice called softly.

The filly opened her eyes. Yellow light filled her stall, not daylight, but lantern light. It was dead of night. She felt a gentle hand on her hindquarters and moved over, looking back. She saw, coming up on her left, the boy she knew so well and loved so deeply. But something had happened to his face. It was painted black.

He walked up to her head, patting her and talking quietly. "Hear me, mighty horse," he whispered into her ear. "The time has come for Stephen Seven Trees to go off and seek his spirit dream. I'll be back in three or four days. Good-by, Lady Suffolk. Good-by, mighty horse. Wait for me!"

The lantern went out, the darkness closed in, and the boy was gone.

9

A BUTCHER'S HORSE

"Dog? Come down here, you Montauk rascal! Think you can sleep all day?"

The horse dealer stood at the foot of the ladder, shouting up into the loft. His upper lip was puffed out, and both cheeks had deep scratches, as if raked by claws. The barn was filled with light. From the pasture, the good, clean smell of dewy grass and the wide-awake calls of birds came on the early morning breeze. Lady Suffolk was ready for her breakfast. From the snorts and stamping that sounded in the other stalls, so were the other horses.

"Dog! Get that dirty hide of yours down here. You've got chores!"

"What's the hubbub?" the housekeeper asked from the barn door. She had a black eye.

"The hubbub, madam, if it's any concern of yours, which I doubt, has to do with a filthy Indian boy who has been taking advantage of my generous nature for the past two years and who has suddenly decided that he can sleep all day. Dog!"

Sensing her loss for the first time, the filly gave a long, sad neigh.

With the greatest difficulty because of his stiff right knee, the dealer began to climb the rungs of the ladder—one at a time, pulling his right leg up behind him like a log.

"I expect you might have some regrets about your conduct in this little matter when we meet," he muttered almost to himself. "I ain't a Johnny Cake, I ain't. . . . He's gone!"

"He can't be!" Mrs. Eller exclaimed.

"Are you calling me a liar, madam?" Billings snarled down from the loft. A rapid thumping sounded from the boards overhead, as the dealer limped around up there. His whispery voice had a note of despair, unusual for him, when he said, "Gone, and everything with him!"

"Oh, Stephen!" the housekeeper cried. "You didn't even say good-by!"

Slowly, awkwardly, the dealer came down the ladder, his right leg seeming to be an enormous weight that he could barely manage. At the bottom, he turned to the housekeeper and demanded, "Did you ever see that wolf pelt Dog had?"

"I did."

"Did you ever see what was in it?"

"The knife, you mean, and the little jars—"

"You know what I'm talking about madam—the wampum, the belt of beads."

Lady Suffolk felt the tension between the two humans as strongly as if she knew that Little Billy was about to pay her his respects. She snorted, shifting her weight uneasily.

"Mrs. Eller," Billings whispered, "it would please me

if you would answer my question. *Did you see the wampum?*"

"I did."

"Do you know what it means?"

"I do not."

The dealer was watching Lady Suffolk closely with his sunken blue eyes. She gave a nervous whinny.

"Did Dog, by any chance, leave the wolf pelt and its contents in your care?"

"No, Mr. Billings, he did not."

"Are you telling me the truth?"

"I have never lied to you, sir."

The dealer smacked his gloved hands together in exasperation. "He's not coming back!" After a thoughtful pause, he added, "Funny, I had reckoned he was so fond of the filly that he wouldn't leave her—only reason I've kept her as long as I have. Why didn't he take her with him, I wonder?"

"Because, Mr. Billings, Stephen is not a thief."

The dealer glanced at her in surprise. At last he replied, "Dog is an Indian, and all Indians are thieves."

"That's not true about Indians, and Stephen is also your sister's child," Mrs. Eller reminded him.

"In any event, not another day will that filly stay here," the dealer told her.

"And not another day will I," the housekeeper replied.

Billings stared at her in amazement. "What are you talking about?"

"I am leaving your employ."

"You can't, madam! You've been with me seven years!"

"Seems like twenty."

"But you just can't!"

"I can and I am—today, now."

"But *why*?"

"I expect you know why, Mr. Billings."

"Not because I'm selling Lady Suffolk!"

At the sound of her name the filly pricked up her ears.

"No, no, no!"

"Why then? Because of our little disagreement last night? That was nothing, madam, *nothing*. You must know that I didn't mean to hit you. You woke me from a sound sleep when you came into my room, and I struck out by instinct. In any event, from all appearances, you got the better end of that tussle," he added, gingerly feeling his face.

The housekeeper was silent.

"Mrs. Eller, I do believe it is the concern of Bill Billings if Billings cares to wear his gloves to bed. I do not believe it is the concern of Mrs. James W. Eller or anyone else in these United States."

The silence became stony.

"I believe that Billings was within his rights in protecting his privacy when you tried to take the gloves off, Mrs. Eller. Madam, will you speak? Are you afflicted with the same ailment that the half-blood suffered from—Montauk lockjaw?"

"Mr. Billings," she said at last, "what happened last night has nothing to do with my leaving. As Stephen has gone, so must I go."

"*Stephen*? You can't love that dirty, stupid redskin!"

"Mr. Billings, do you realize that that is the first time you have ever called your nephew by his right name? Well, he's half Montauk, that's true, but he's far from stupid, and he's a nation cleaner than *somebody I* know."

"But you can't love him, madam!"

The housekeeper's voice was soft. "I wouldn't say I *loved* Stephen," she replied. "He was awfully hard to get to know. I was right fond of the boy, though, particularly toward the end. Stephen's the only reason I've stayed on here the past two years. And now that he's gone, there's no reason for me to stay."

"But what will you do, Mrs. Eller? Positions are not so easy to find these days. You might not be aware of it, but the republic is suffering from a depression. Aye, these United States are in a sorry state of affairs—banks closing, factories shutting down. And we thought matters were bad under Jackson! Of course, Van Buren is just Old Hickory's puppet, but you'd think that there would be enough brains between the two of them to annex Texas, wouldn't you?"

The stony silence prevailed.

"Remember the Alamo! Aye, but it appears that both of them have forgotten it already. Davy Crockett, Jim Bowie, and a hundred and eighty other brave men gave their lives —and to what end?"

If the dealer were asking a question, Mrs. Eller wasn't answering.

"I saw Crockett, you know, when the Whigs sent him through these parts a few years back," Billings went on. "Tall, lanky man, with long, dark hair, dressed in buckskin. You know what he told Daniel Webster? 'I heard you were a very great man,' says Crockett. 'But I don't think so,' says he. Says he, 'I heard your speech and understood every word of it.' "

Then came Billings' reedy laugh that sounded to Lady Suffolk like the neigh of a very old horse. From the house-keeper came no sound at all. After a long silence, she said, "I must go."

"Then go, madam. Go! You owe me half a month's wages, but that's all right."

"The exact amount will be on the kitchen table."

"Go then. Leave me. I never could abide your cooking, anyhow. I'll get a young girl at half what I paid you. Mrs. Eller, it's been seven years! You can't just walk out. Listen, if it's so important that you see my hands, I'll show them to you. I'll take my gloves off right now."

"I have no more interest in the matter, Mr. Billings."

"There's nothing to see, really. I have a mark on my left thumb, a scar curved in the shape of 'HT' for Hoover's Tavern. There was a bunch of us who used to run together in Tennessee, a club you might call it, and we hung out at this wilderness inn outside Nashville called Hoover's Tavern. Everyone in the club had the 'HT' carved on his thumb. It was a bit of foolishness, I'll grant you, but we were all young and—"

"Mr. Billings, you are a liar."

"*Liar* am I? Here, I'll show you."

"Get out of my way." The housekeeper's voice was low but full of menace.

Pulling his glove back on, the dealer stepped aside, and Mrs. Eller walked out of the barn. Neither of them said good-by.

*   *   *

That afternoon, Billings came back into the barn with another man. They walked up to Lady Suffolk's stall. She recognized the dealer's companion—he was the burly man in the floppy hat who had been present when the little yellow dog had made Waterloo bolt last winter.

"She hasn't grown much since I saw her last, I'll be bound," the man remarked to Billings.

"She's a big little one, long for her inches, Mr. Mercer, and she's every day a-coming," the dealer replied. "Look at that head. That's where you judge an animal's breeding, spirit, and way of going, sir. You see how finely drawn it is, the bones prominent, the lines clean cut. Note the wide-set eyes—that shows intelligence. Beware the horse with a large bump over the eyes. That indicates too much brain and therefore craftiness."

The burly man hunched his shoulders and said, "I just want a horse to pull my meat wagon."

"This is the horse for you, sir. She's the best that ever looked through a bridle, she is. She's made of whalebone and wire. This horse is like a steel spring. The harder you bear upon it, the greater the force of the rebound. You just try to wear this horse out, sir. You just try!"

"I've worn out a few in my time," the butcher said with no little pride.

"The good Lord put them on this earth to work," the dealer told him.

"That's why he put *us* here," Mercer replied. "This horse is smaller than most," he went on. "You reckon she could pull a meat wagon?"

"Pull a meat wagon!" Billings exclaimed. "Indeed she could, and all day long. You know the old saying: 'She

can't go fast enough to tire herself.' You just try to wear
her out, sir!''

"A meat wagon is a heavy wagon," Mercer told Billings.
"And I deliver all over the Island, including the North
Shore, where there are hills a-plenty."

"Hills!" the dealer snorted. *"Mountains* might present
a problem to Lady Suffolk—although I doubt it seriously—
but hills are as nothing to her. Those legs are cast iron.
Trace that fine, well-set neck, those powerful shoulders,
that strong, straight back, the long barrel, well ribbed-up,
powerful forearms, fine pasterns—"

"Enough! Enough!" The butcher threw up his hands.
"I just want a horse to pull my meat wagon."

David Mercer was not tall, but he was broad. His shoulders were bullish and his legs were bowed like barrel staves
from carrying sides of pork and beef to and from his
wagon. He had impressive jaw muscles as the result of
nearly a half-century of chewing vast quantities of his
product at breakfast, dinner, and supper, with a snack before bed, seven days a week, 365 days a year.

"Every man must go to the devil by his own road," the
dealer said. "But if you will take the advice of Bill Billings, you'll buy this horse before somebody else beats you
to it, yes, sir."

Mercer made a big show of looking all about him. "I
don't see *too* many buyers waiting."

"Never fear, sir, I'll have no trouble selling this horse,
even with the desperate situation the republic is in today—
our gold and silver flowing out of the country to Europe,
prices going up, and up. It's not the big bugs that suffer,
of course, it's us little fellows."

The butcher hunched his shoulders, repeating gruffly, "Us little fellows?"

"The workies, aye, the farmers, the laborers, the mechanics, the small businessmen like you and me, aye, the bone and sinew of the nation. We're the ones who suffer. These United States are in a bad way, sir. The flour riot in the city in February, that's a sign of what's in store for us. It was the Paris mob, screaming for bread, that started the French Revolution, you know."

"The French Revolution, I'll be bound," Mercer said. "They had one too?" He hunched his shoulders, remarking testily, "I'm looking for a horse to pull my meat wagon. Are you interested in selling this one?"

"I am indeed, sir."

"Well, let's get on with it then," Mercer replied. He took Lady Suffolk by the nose in his big, badly scarred butcher's hands and studied every mark on her teeth. Then he lifted each hoof and stared at it as if it had insulted him. He hunched his shoulders and huffed.

"She's a big little one, long for her inches, and she's every day a-coming," the dealer told him.

"You said that," Mercer remarked in his gruff manner.

"Let us go into the house and discuss terms over a cup of coffee or perhaps something more lighthearted," the dealer suggested.

The butcher's gruffness was gone in an instant. "A capital suggestion, Billings," he said, clapping the other man on the back with enough force to stagger him. "I'm bone dry, I'll be bound."

When they returned to the barn, a good while later, it was obvious from their bright eyes that they had not done their bargaining over coffee. Both were smiling on the off-side of their faces, well satisfied that they had made a good deal. The butcher brought Lady Suffolk out of her stall and tied her to the axle of his buggy. Climbing in, he clucked to his horse, a rangy black mare, and she started off at a brisk trot, the filly following behind. Mercer and Billings exchanged cordial farewells. Rushing once more into the unknown, Lady Suffolk gave a long, sad whinny for the boy she missed so sorely and another for herself.

10

TO SETTLE AN OLD SCORE

"You just try to wear this horse out," Billings had said, and the butcher did his best. All David Mercer knew in life was work. When he wasn't working, the butcher felt ill at ease, almost guilty. He worked so hard that at night he toppled into bed like a tree felled in a forest and slept a dreamless sleep until he started another workday. As a result of his sentiment, he loathed Sunday and dreaded its arrival, starting about Wednesday afternoon of each workweek, pushing himself and his horse ever harder until, by Saturday, there was nothing but toil and moil from sunup to sundown.

After church Sunday, he spent the day moping around the house, twiddling his mighty thumbs, drumming his scarred fingers, and glumly watching his wife cook the roast beef, ham, liver, chops, sausages, and fixings that usually made up Sunday dinner. He could have gone out in the backyard and chopped wood, but this was one of his son's chores, and for the butcher to do it would be in the nature

of recreation and therefore taboo. In the same way, although there were streams and ponds near their home,
Mercer refused to let his son swim in them, for, as he explained, "When you're swimming, you're not working."

To the butcher, Lady Suffolk was a challenge. It seemed
he could not give her too much work, but he kept trying,
taking the greatest pride in the way she responded, bragging about her strength to his wife and son, and the men
he knew at work. To him and everyone else who would
listen, she was made of "whalebone and wire," with "cast
iron legs."

He was not stingy with her feed, giving her as many as
twelve and sometimes thirteen quarts of oats a day, but the
work he put her to easily burned them up. She never had
quite enough food and never nearly enough rest.

The ache of her muscles, ligaments and bones, however,
was nothing to the ache inside her, from an emptiness that
had once swelled with love for a boy—a boy who had a
special whistle for her, who used to share his apples with
her, who chanted to her and mimicked her trot, and sometimes even got down on his hands and knees in the pasture
and grazed with her. That lean, dark-haired boy belonged
to a long time ago, and the mists of time were closing in.
But the aching emptiness remained in the chest of Lady
Suffolk as the next several years passed in dreary succession
and she was no longer a filly but a mare.

The yearning pain was worst by far in the spring. Then
every bee, cricket, frog, bird, and squirrel, by its individual
sound, and every flower and blossom, by its scent, recalled
that old happy time when she and the boy were together.

Hauling a wagon full of oysters and clams or sides of

beef and pork, Lady Suffolk trotted around Long Island, through the driving rains of spring, the oven heat of summer, the falling leaves and gray mists of autumn, and the blinding snows of winter. Whatever the season, she constantly encountered other horses and drivers whose happy-go-lucky air seemed out of place in her workaday world. But her grim trade made her each day a bit stronger, a bit tougher.

"No two ways about it," the butcher remarked to his wife and son repeatedly, "that gray mare is the toughest piece of horseflesh that ever looked through a bridle. Whalebone and wire, I'll be bound."

The hills of the North Shore gave her trouble. To haul a heavily loaded wagon up a hill was bad enough, but the trip back down—with the wagon rumbling like a landslide at her heels, threatening to roll over her—was a horror. The butcher did his part by putting blocks in front of the wheels to slow the wagon down, and by using the whip.

As dedicated as he appeared to the practice, David Mercer received no pleasure from flogging horses. He did it just as he went to church on Sunday, because he thought that that was what you did, no two ways about it. To him, the whip was a tool that played as important a part in the working of a horse as the reins and the bridle.

He learned differently one winter afternoon in the second year of Lady Suffolk's servitude—although he soon forgot the lesson. It was a particularly mean day, with the wind out of the west, driving sullen, dark clouds like a herd of ill-tempered bulls before it. The workload had been heavier than usual, and Lady Suffolk was more worn out than usual, so she was not in complete command of herself.

They were on their way home when she heard a merry jingle of bells behind her. Then a chestnut mare, with vapor smoking from her nostrils in the frosty air, pranced by. She was pulling a sleigh in which sat a young man and a girl, both wearing fur coats, fur gloves, and fur hats, and snuggling under a heavy fur rug, so that they might have been a couple of bears, except for their red, wind-bitten faces. The sleigh passed on the left, within a few inches of Lady Suffolk, the runners shrieking on the hard-packed snow. Startled, the little gray mare shied to the right—onto a stretch of ice that lay hidden under the snow.

Her feet shot out from under her, her legs flew up, the world gave a mad twist, and she crashed on the ice. (The furry young man and girl never looked back.) The fall knocked the wind out of Lady Suffolk and stunned her for several seconds. But when her brain cleared, she became filled with terror, an instinctive fear that went back millions of years. A fallen horse was just so many pounds of meat and gnawing bones to wolves, lions, bears—any predators that happened by. She *had* to get to her feet.

Lady Suffolk struggled to rise, but her legs were like stilts and her smooth shoes slipped on the ice as if they had been greased. She fell, fought to get up again, and fell once more, continuing the futile battle until she was exhausted. Then she lay between the shafts of the wagon, her chest swelling and contracting as she breathed the keen air, trying to work up her strength to renew the fight.

So filled had she been with the fear of prowling wolves and other shadowy killers that she had been unaware that the butcher had been whipping her ever since she had fallen. Now she felt the long, cruel welts as he stood up in the wagon and sent the lash down upon her again and again, the stern tool swishing through the air and landing on her flesh with a loud *whomp*. Mercer was flogging her, not out of anger, but because he sincerely believed the whip would help her get up.

Some minutes before he beat her unconscious, the butcher stopped. His powerful arm was tired, for one thing, and for another he saw that the tool had failed to do what he had expected of it. About this time, the sullen clouds overhead opened up and a hard, frigid rain came down like the waves of a stormy sea.

The mare resumed the struggle to rise, but her feet continued to fail her. Mercer stood in the rain, watching the uneven contest. Then he took off his overcoat and spread it under her hoofs.

"Come along, Lady Suffolk," he told her in his gruff manner.

Holding her bridle, he pulled steadily, walking backwards. Lady Suffolk tried anew, and, this time, her hoofs took hold on the coat. She was on her feet, her entire body atremble, but she was on her feet!

"Go ahead," the butcher told her, without adding the whip.

He drove her down the road some distance before he stopped her and ran back to get his overcoat. That night, he gave the mare an extra quart of oats—and it was nearly two weeks before he used the whip on her again.

* * *

One day the following spring, Lady Suffolk performed a feat that really gave the butcher something to brag about, a deed that dramatically changed the course of the little gray mare's life. Several factors played a part in the situation. For one thing, it was Monday morning, after a day of rest—a warm, sunny morn, following a chilly night—and Lady Suffolk was in fine fettle, her morale better than it had been in years. For another thing, the meat wagon was empty; Mercer was driving to an icehouse in Jamaica to load up.

They were traveling along Jamaica Turnpike at a smart pace when it happened. From some distance ahead sounded the blare of a trumpet. *Er-r-r-rah, er-r-r-rah!*

Lady Suffolk's ears pricked up. She hadn't heard that call in ages. It was also the first time the notes had sounded that Little Billy didn't immediately enter the picture. With no encouragement from the butcher, she began to trot faster. He did not understand why; but, since she was working, he let her have her way. Although they were climbing a long hill, the speed of her trot kept building, her legs moving in a fine, quick stroke, the knees bending well.

Er-r-r-rah, er-r-r-rah! Ta-ta-tah!

They reached the top of the hill. The road curved off to the right. Just disappearing around the bend was the stage-coach, the buggy swaying like a hammock in its leather sling. Trotting ever faster, Lady Suffolk thrust out her long slender neck like a wild goose in flight, her full tail flowing behind her. As she rounded the bend, the stage again came into view. It was about a hundred yards ahead.

Then it vanished again, when the road dipped into a dismal hollow and became corduroy. The wheels of the meat wagon rattled over the logs as the mare dashed by the dark trees that stood gloomily in a pond on each side of the road, or leaned upon each other as if exhausted, or lay down as though having given up completely. Then the foliage ahead was shot through with shafts of sunlight, and, quickly, she was out of the hollow—and there was the stage-coach, fifty yards ahead.

Forty. Lady Suffolk's four gray legs were flashing in neat precision, driving like pistons, as she trotted low to the ground, her head straight out, her tail streaming back in the breeze she made as her hoofs drummed along the road. Thirty yards.

Her bright eyes were fastened on the swinging stage. Perhaps sensing the intense gaze, a passenger stuck his head out the window and saw her coming up. His mouth popped open. Reaching above with an umbrella, he hammered on the side of the stage to get the driver's attention, then shouted something to him.

Other passengers stuck their heads out of the window to see the oncoming gray mare, but the driver kept his back turned. His long whip cracked over his four horses' heads like pistol shots. They were galloping, as they had been all along, but now they strained themselves to the utmost, and the lather flew from them in globs.

Lady Suffolk, however, could not be denied. She was twenty-five yards behind the stagecoach. Twenty. Pebbles thrown back by the stage's spinning wheels and the hoofs of the team pelted the gray mare and the butcher, and rattled on the front of the meat wagon. The mare and her master were almost blinded and smothered in the cloud of dust.

The stage was fifteen yards away. The windows on both sides sprouted with the big round faces of the passengers as they watched the mare's approach in amazement. The driver had never looked back, but his whip was exploding steadily over his horses' heads, and he gave a despairing blast on his trumpet.

Ten yards. Drumming, rumbling, the racers crossed a bridge of loose planks over a brown stream that was slowly turning the wheel of a flour mill. They were approaching a community of small white houses. A church steeple rose above the foliage of the shady trees, and a little red school-house shot by. A short distance ahead was a two-story frame building, the Mill Creek Inn, the stagecoach's destination; and the driver made for it desperately, in hopes he could reach it before the mare passed him.

The arrival of the stage was an important event, and a crowd was gathered outside the inn, waiting to get the latest news. The long porch was lined with guests in rocking chairs, rocking. Boys were running toward the inn from a nearby field, holding the strings of kites that bounced through the sky behind them. Dogs were barking, roosters crowing. Pigs—self-confident, self-centered, self-satisfied porkers—glanced up from their cozy mudholes where they had been taking their ease by the side of the road and grunted in surprise as the two contenders thundered past.

The little gray mare, still in her neat, rhythmical trot, came up on the stagecoach and began to pass it, hoof by hoof, to the utter consternation of the passengers, whose

round, red faces bloomed like geraniums in the windows. She trotted by the driver, a tall, bony man with a deeply creased, leathery face, burned by the sun, whipped by the wind, and beaten by rain, sleet, snow, and hail. Stuck around the inside of his black beaverskin stovepipe hat were the edges of receipts and letters he was to deliver. He never once glanced down at the mare, but kept his eyes straight ahead, focused on the inn. The rockers on the porch and the crowd in the front yard began to cheer.

"Huzza for the gray! Go it, little horse!"

The acclaim roared in Lady Suffolk's ears and acted like adrenalin in her body, making her trot even faster. She came up to the hindquarters of the first pair of horses, then, steadily passed their barrels, shoulders, necks, heads. Trotting like a well-oiled machine, she slipped by the second pair. All four were white with lather and wild-eyed. If they could have kicked her, they would have gladly; to bite her would have given them the keenest pleasure.

There were thirty yards of daylight between the rear of the meat wagon and the whistling noses of the first pair of stagecoach horses when the poker-faced driver—still pretending that his was the only vehicle on the road and that he always drove in such a crazed manner—pulled up at the Mill Creek Inn.

The little gray mare continued down the road at the same rate, as if she had no other speed than the flying trot. For the first time in years—ever since the boy had left— Lady Suffolk found life sweet.

11

THE CHALLENGE

"Toughest piece of horseflesh that ever looked through a bridle, I'll be bound."

This was perhaps the five hundredth time that the butcher had made the observation, but he spoke the words now as though they had just come to him. He was ad dressing a crowd of idlers in the front yard of the Mill Creek Inn.

It was nearing the end of a warm spring day, a few weeks after Lady Suffolk had vanquished the stagecoach. Mercer had stopped at the inn to water the mare and treat himself to other refreshment of a liquid nature, since he was, as he remarked to his friend, the innkeeper, "bone dry."

He was quite a bit moister when he came out of the inn, two hours later, and in a bragging mood. He found the crowd admiring Lady Suffolk, who stood quietly between the shafts of the meat wagon. The day had been hard, although not unusually arduous, and she was enjoying the rest. The fifteen gallons of water she had taken aboard while waiting for her master had helped to revive her considerably.

"No two ways about it, she's all whalebone and wire," the butcher remarked, again managing to lend a certain freshness to the expression.

A tall, bony man at the edge of the crowd was watching him with something of a sneer on his deeply creased, leathery face. To emphasize his statement, Mercer slapped the mare on the shoulder. She took it docilely. A slap was better than a lash, any day.

One of the idlers faced the crowd and pointed dramatically to the earth at his feet.

"I was standing right here, and I saw the whole affair," he announced. "That stage came dashing up the road, all four horses galloping. And this little mare here passed them like they were standing still. And she was trotting, mind you. *Trotting*. I saw the whole affair. Standing right here."

Pointing to Lady Suffolk's chest, another exclaimed, "Mark that front! I don't know that I've ever seen one broader, with muscles so well defined."

He added to his neighbor, "A narrow front means poor staying power."

"She has game and bottom, if I know anything about horseflesh," the other man replied. "She'd have to. Those stage horses are nigh impossible to beat, even for a horse going under saddle. It must have taken the mare a couple of miles to catch them."

"Almost any horse can pull a moderate weight over a good road," the first man said. "But the horse that can draw much more than five hundred pounds for two miles in anything under six minutes is scarce indeed."

The crowd nodded assent, and there were several "Yes, sir's."

Holding up his big hand for silence, Mercer coolly announced, "Lady Suffolk could do it in under five and a half minutes."

Silence Mercer wanted and silence he got. In the hush that followed his announcement, the idlers exchanged glances that were a mixture of awe and doubt. Then the tall, bony man stepped forward. The sneer was unmistakable now.

"Do *what?*" he demanded.

"Why, pull my wagon two miles in under five and a half minutes, to be sure," the butcher replied, somewhat surprised at the other man's aggressive manner.

"*This* wagon?" the sneerer asked.

"This wagon," Mercer agreed.

"As it stands?"

"As it stands."

"From a dead stop?"

"From a dead stop."

"With you driving?"

"With me driving, of course," Mercer replied. "Who else?"

There was something familiar about the other man, but the butcher couldn't place him.

The innkeeper, Edmund Trowbridge, who had come out from the parlor, took a careful look inside the wagon.

"Dave!" he exclaimed. "You've got a good five hundred pounds of beef hanging in there!"

Although his face showed no emotion, Mercer's heart

sank. He had completely forgotten about those two sides
of beef that he had not yet delivered. He felt dazed. His
face was hot with the blood that had flooded into it.
Loosened by the refreshment he had imbibed during the
past two hours, his tongue felt stiff and over-sized in a
mouth that now was truly bone dry.

He watched stupidly as the idlers trooped to the back of
the wagon, peered in, and came away shaking their heads.

"Man, man," the innkeeper exclaimed, "do you realize
that between you and the wagon and the meat, that little
horse would be pulling more than eleven hundred
pounds?"

Mercer gave an airy wave of his hand. "I agree with my
English friends. The amount of weight that the horse pulls
makes no difference in its speed."

Ed Trowbridge snorted. "That's next kin to nonsense,
and you well know it."

Mercer did. As cool as he acted, he was appalled at his
stupid brag. Eleven hundred pounds! He was a fool, no
two ways about that. He suspected that the bony man had
been lying in wait for him to make some outlandish claim
for Lady Suffolk, and he had walked right into the trap
with his stupid eyes wide open.

Eleven hundred pounds—more! His little gray mare, as
strong as she was, as plucky as she was, would have to be
a superhorse to pull that awful load two miles in the time
he had given her. . . .

From the spreading sneer on his face, the bony man had
obviously checked the contents of the wagon before the
butcher had even started his boasting. That extra five hundred pounds could make all the difference. Something else,

Lady Suffolk was not fresh. Mercer could tell from her heavy breathing that she was tired.

The butcher's confused gaze went from face to face in the crowd. In some he saw sympathy; others showed as much emotion as a tree, a stone. From their sly smiles, a few men were enjoying his predicament.

Anger built up in the butcher, driving the blood through his veins. And the man that made him the maddest was the tall, bony fellow who had just clapped on his black stovepipe hat. The corner of a letter that he had failed to deliver stuck out from it, over one ear.

Of course! He was the driver of the stagecoach that Lady Suffolk had defeated.

"Now then, about this famous mare . . ." The stage driver was addressing the butcher, but his eyes were sweeping the crowd. "Are you telling the good gentlemen here that she *could* perform the deed, or *can*?"

David Mercer hunched his shoulders. "*Can*, to be sure, and *will*!"

"Now?" his antagonist asked softly.

"Now."

The stage driver reached into his coat and pulled out a purse, which he held high, for all to see. "Here's two hundred and fifty dollars—hard money—that says she can't!"

"I'm not carrying that much," the butcher told him.

"Well, then, I expect you were just exercising your jaw," the stage driver remarked. "Would you care to take back what you said this little mare could do?"

The butcher glared at the other man, and hunched his shoulders again. "You'll get no crawfishing or sidestepping or pulling in of horns, not from *me*, you won't! He turned to the innkeeper. "I've got fifty, Ed. Can you lend me the two hundred?"

"I can, Dave, of course . . ." Trowbridge's tone left a "but" hanging in the warm spring afternoon air. No one else spoke. Aware of the tension, Lady Suffolk shifted her weight nervously. The two-hour rest, following her extended workout, had stiffened her muscles to a degree.

"Well, gents, what's your pleasure?" the stage driver demanded impatiently.

Without a word, although his long, pale face was filled with deep mourning, Ed Trowbridge produced his own purse, counted out two hundred dollars in clinking silver, and handed the money to his friend. The butcher added his own fifty.

"Mr. Culley, would you be good enough to hold the stakes?" the innkeeper asked a man who had been standing quietly in the background. Ford Culley was a well-built individual of medium height whose wavy brown beard showed traces of gray. He agreed to hold the money— and appeared to grow bigger from the attention he received.

"From here to the Mill Creek School, around the flagpole, and back is two miles even," the stage driver told Mercer.

The butcher glanced at Trowbridge, who nodded his agreement.

"Remember now, butcher," the stage driver added, "this time you're racing a clock. You're not chasing horses that are at the end of their run and dead beat from hauling a coach and six of the largest gentry in the republic."

"They weren't dead beat until this little mare dead beat them," the butcher snapped.

"Care to raise our little bet?" the stage driver asked softly.

Mercer glanced at Trowbridge, who shook his head lugubriously, and the sneer on the stage driver's face broadened.

The crowd of idlers shrank to almost nothing as the younger men went to fetch their parents, brothers and sisters, and the older men went for their wives and children, and every crack rushed to get his horse and buggy.

Within a few minutes, the entire population of Mill Creek, a community of about three hundred souls, was assembled in the front yard of the inn and along both sides of the road leading to the school.

Long odds were being offered against Lady Suffolk, but there were few takers. The load was too heavy, the distance too far, the time too short, and the mare too small for anyone but the most reckless gambler to be tempted.

"She's smaller than I would have thought," a man remarked. "I don't believe she would go fifteen hands."

"She's a big little one, long for her inches, and she's every day a-coming," Mercer said, back to bragging again and getting some consolation from it.

Another man crouched down and began to measure the mare with the width of his hand, going up one foreleg to her withers. He faced the crowd:

"Fifteen even."

"Weighs no more than a thousand pounds, I'd say," the first man remarked.

"Whalebone and wire, every bit of it," the butcher said.

"I put her at eleven hundred," the measurer announced.

"Whalebone and wire, I'll be bound," Mercer added.

"She's in good fix, I'll say that," the measurer told the crowd. The "Yes, sir's" were many and loud.

Lady Suffolk's ears were cocked. She did not know what the men were saying, but she sensed their admiring tone. She certainly was in good fix. Her dappled gray coat was sleek and glossy. Her eyes were bright and eager. Her nostrils flared like the bell of a bugle.

She heard the buzz of low talk from the crowd. Everyone's excitement and anticipation affected her, and she stamped her feet, snorting impatiently.

Something involving her, she sensed, was about to happen, and she was anxious to get going. She was champing at the bit.

"Four to one she don't make it!" someone shouted. There were no takers.

"Five to one!" Still no takers.

"Whalebone and wire," the butcher said.

The innkeeper pulled Mercer aside.

"Dave, you have both sides of beef hanging on the left," he told the butcher quietly. "It would give the wagon a better balance if you had one on each side."

"You're right," Mercer replied and climbed into the wagon.

"Hold!" the stage driver ordered. "Just what is it that you think you're about, if I may ask?"

"I'm not taking anything out," Mercer told him. "I'm just rearranging my meat."

"That you're not!" the stage driver replied. "The agreement, if I recall correctly, was the wagon 'as it stands,' and that's the way it stands."

"Listen now," Trowbridge began, his long face flaming with anger.

"The wagon *'as it stands,'* " the stage driver repeated emphatically.

Mercer shrugged his shoulders and climbed down from the wagon.

"When you get to the flagpole, go around it on the right, so the weight of the beef is on the *inside,*" Trowbridge told his friend in a low tone. "Otherwise you might tip over."

Mercer nodded.

"Well, butcher, can we get on with it?" The stage driver's voice had an edge.

The excited buzz of talk from the crowd had been growing steadily louder and more impatient. Behind the meat wagon was a long line of dandies, each in his buggy. A number of men were going in the saddle. The horses were stamping and snorting nervously.

Mercer and his antagonist selected a trio of men from the crowd to act as judges. Then the stage driver swung into the saddle of a horse that was as bony as he was, explaining with his customary sneer, "I just want to be sure everything goes along all right."

Trowbridge shook hands with Mercer as if both were about to be hanged.

"Good luck, Dave," the innkeeper told his friend in his lugubrious way. "Remember, go around the flagpole on the right."

"Now for it!" the butcher remarked with feigned enthusiasm as he climbed into the wagon.

A hush fell over the crowd. Everyone was watching the judges. The only sounds were the snorts and stampings of the horses. Lady Suffolk could feel the excitement building up in her—building up and building up with each passing second.

The middle judge, a man in a gray top hat, raised his right hand, index finger extended like a dueling pistol. His eyes were on the watch in the palm of his left hand. After an agonizing pause, he swung the finger down.

"Go!" he shouted.

"Go ahead!" the butcher ordered, cracking the whip over Lady Suffolk's ears. She lunged forward, the harness tightening around her chest, the heavy wagon rumbling behind her as she stepped out—left foreleg and right hindleg, right foreleg and left hindleg—clop, clop, clop, clop, in a long, low sweeping stroke.

"Go it, Lady Suffolk!" the crowd roared, and "Huzza for the little gray mare!" There were also many "Yes, sir's!"

Behind the butcher's wagon, the long line of buggies and horsemen shot forward, making it appear that Lady Suffolk was leading a grand exodus out of Mill Creek. Her legs swinging in perfect rhythm, the little gray mare rushed past the high row of excited older faces, the lower row of even more excited younger faces, and, below them, the absolutely astounded bristly faces of pigs that stared out from their mud domains along both sides of the road.

The mare's stiffness was gone and she was trotting well, her knees bending nicely. She was making excellent time, and she had not begun to tire—yet. Beside her, the stage driver rode his bony mount. Through the trees ahead, the mare saw the little red schoolhouse, the flagpole standing in front of it. The stage driver saw it, too. He glared at his watch, then held it tight to his ear to be sure it was still ticking.

He pulled his horse within just a few inches of Lady Suffolk, obviously trying to make her bolt or break her stride.

"Stay clear!" the butcher roared, but his antagonist refused to withdraw until threatened with the whip.

The crowd was far behind. The only noise was the clopping of hoofs. So many hoofs there were that they sounded like a cavalry charge or a stampede, along with the rumble and rattle of wheels. The flagpole was dead ahead, with a smooth dirt road circling it.

Mercer pulled the mare's left rein, directing her around the left side of the pole. Halfway around it, she felt a sharp pain in the mouth as her master yanked on the reins, having remembered too late that he should have gone around the other side of the pole.

The wagon, with its five hundred pounds of beef hanging on the left side, tipped so that it ran on two wheels and was in grave danger of toppling over completely.

Mercer snarled in anger. There were cries of dismay from the men and women following behind. The stage driver's long yellow teeth showed in a triumphant grin. The meat wagon kept rolling along on two wheels for several long, crazy seconds, then rocked back on all four. But Lady Suffolk had broken her stride and was running in a confused, jerky gait that ate up the time. She had circled the flagpole and was heading back along the road toward the Mill Creek Inn.

Exhaustion suddenly settled upon her like a heavy

blanket. Her hoofs were leaden and her legs were beginning to stiffen. Her breathing was labored. Nonetheless, she passed out of her awkward gait into the clean, even, low, locomotive-drive stroke of before. She raced for the distant inn, thrusting her long neck out, her tail flowing behind her.

That is when Mercer, in his frenzy, began to use the whip. This bewildered her and made her break her stride a second time. Many more precious seconds were lost and the wagon was moving much more slowly than before.

"You might as well give up, butcher!" the stage driver shouted. "You'll never make it now!"

"Watch me!" Mercer replied.

He had the presence of mind to stop whipping Lady Suffolk. Once more, she was able to collect herself and slip into a trot, but each step took a little more out of her, and the wagon that rumbled grimly behind her seemed to be loaded with iron. The breath whistled in and out of her nostrils, and her sides were covered with lather. Her head felt too heavy for her neck. Behind her, she could hear the groans of disappointment from the horsemen and occupants of the buggies. The stage driver gave a gleeful chuckle.

Up ahead, the crowd had pushed out into the road, everyone straining to see the little gray mare.

"Here she is! Come along, Lady Suffolk! Huzza! Huzza!"

The mare's head raised, her ears pricked up, her nostrils flared. The hurricane roar of the crowd, which grew steadily louder and wilder, seemed to flow through her body, driving out the exhaustion and pain, bringing in strength. Her trot became neater, more rhythmical, faster.

Now she was passing between the people, who pressed in from both sides of the road. The men were waving their hats, the women were fluttering their handkerchiefs, and everyone was screaming. The Mill Creek Inn was just a short distance ahead.

"What's the time?" Mercer yelled.

Several told him, but the cheers drowned out the replies.

"What's the time?" he shouted again.

"Five minutes, twenty seconds!" a leather-lunged man yelled, cupping his hands around his mouth to funnel the words. "Go it, Lady Suffolk! You can do it!"

The mare was nearly at the inn. Men, women and children lined the long porch. Five twenty-five. The judges had drawn a line across the dirt in the road by the front yard. Five twenty-seven. Lady Suffolk gave the last bit of strength and pluck she had. Something inside her tore and she stumbled—but she pulled the meat wagon across the finish line.

The crowd, so uproarious just seconds before, was silent as the three judges compared their watches and conferred, nodding gravely in the manner of judges, whether professional or amateur. Then the man in the gray top hat stepped forward, paused dramatically and held up his hand for the silence he already had.

"The time," he announced . . . then paused once more as the community of Mill Creek held its breath, "Five minutes and twenty-nine seconds!"

Like a great flock of birds, hats exploded into the air. Men were shaking hands. Women were kissing the men, other women, and the children they could catch. Tears were streaming down many women's cheeks—and even those of some of the men. Everyone was shouting, not yet aware, in all their mad enthusiasm, that they had been witnesses to the start of a legend.

Mercer had climbed down from the wagon and was telling anyone he could get to listen how he had won his race against the clock.

Lady Suffolk stood in the traces, trembling, completely blown. There was a dull pain inside her, and she could taste blood. Her breathing was a terrible thing to hear, and her legs seemed about to collapse. Busy with their celebration, everyone had temporarily forgotten the cause of it, and she stood alone.

"Your stake and winnings, sir," Ford Culley told the butcher, handing him the five hundred dollars. Mercer repaid the innkeeper his two hundred, then turned to the stage driver, whose sneer had been replaced with a scowl.

"And I have something for you," the butcher told him. Mercer's big, scarred fist smacked against the other man's jaw. The stage driver was stretched unconscious on the ground, under his bony horse, his creased, leathery face wearing no expression of any kind now.

"That's for trying to make the mare bolt," Mercer told his antagonist, although the words fell on ears that would be deaf for some time.

A group of men was admiring Lady Suffolk.

"She's a stout puller."

"She's a splendid goer."

"She has game and deep bottom."

"Yes, sir!"

"I expect you would have no interest in selling the mare?" Ford Culley asked Mercer.

"In that you are correct," the butcher replied.

"I would make you a good offer."

"It would have to be a mighty good one, sir, I'll be bound."

"Two hundred dollars."

"Sir," Mercer pointed out, "she just earned me two hundred and *fifty*."

"Two-fifty then."

"Three hundred," the butcher told him.

"Two-seventy-five," Culley said.

"Three hundred is my price," Mercer replied. "You saw what she is capable of."

"Very well, then, three hundred," Culley agreed. "As the good Benjamin Franklin observes in *Poor Richard's Almanac*, 'Time is money,' and I must be on my way."

Well pleased with the bargain, he paid out three hundred dollars, tied Lady Suffolk to the axle of his buggy, and started on his way. She was much too tired to whinny, and in too much pain to care as her stiff legs carried her into still another life. The iron taste of blood was strong in her mouth.

David Mercer, on his part, found it extremely difficult to keep from smiling as he drove his meat wagon home behind a horse borrowed from the innkeeper. . . . Well, why not? His heavy face broke into a wide grin.

Yes, sir, he thought in his slow way, he had won his wild brag—and two hundred and fifty dollars along with it. He had also become the hero of Mill Creek—and those people wouldn't keep that news to themselves. No, indeed, they would not! The word would spread, and he would become famous. Then, too, he had stretched out a most deserving fellow. Finally, he had got rid of the gray mare for a handsome price when she was ruined.

Ford Culley had not seen her stumble, but Mercer had—and knew from the way she acted afterward that she was in bad fix. He was convinced that he had at last achieved what he had thought was impossible. Superhorse she might be—or *had been*, rather—but he had finally been able to give her more work than she could handle.

The thought gave the butcher satisfaction mixed with sadness as he drove home toward the setting sun—and his supper of steak, liver, sausages and fixings.

12

A WHISTLE IN THE NIGHT

Ford Culley owned a livery stable, a business that was the center of the transportation system at this time, for, on land, the usual means of getting about was the horse, either under saddle or, more commonly in the New England and the New York areas, in harness.

The railroad was just beginning to push out onto Long Island. Being new, it was regarded with suspicion by the bravest and with downright fear by the fainthearted. Therefore, to go from one place to another, most people used the horse or, in a pinch, shanks' mare.

The Culley stable, built of whitewashed brick, was bright and well-ventilated, with a red brick floor and heavy oak rafters. In it were a series of chutes to send the feed from the loft to the mangers of the individual horses.

It was kept clean except, of course, for the cobwebs, since they were thought to bring good luck. An old horseshoe, like a rusty U, was nailed over the doorway, in accordance with another belief that it would protect the building from fire. The stable smelled pleasantly of leather, beeswax, and well-groomed horses.

In it were all kinds of horseflesh, from the drowsy old plodders to the speedy roadsters that the cracks demanded. Culley had intended the little gray mare to serve as both roadster and workhorse, but, when he came into the stable the morning after he brought her home, he found her lying down in her stall, unable to rise, dejectedly munching the straw that covered the floor. She was stiff, almost to the point of being petrified, and feverish.

Culley walked to the end of the stable and knocked on a door. "Jerry Bean," he called, "would you come out?"

"Right away," a voice thick with sleep replied.

Several minutes later, the door opened and an elderly Negro man appeared, fighting back a yawn. He looked as if he had been fighting something or a long series of somebodies most of his life. His hair was like cotton. His back was bent as though he were carrying a heavy burden, and his black fingers were gnarled and twisted like the roots of a tree from arthritis. Old, dull-gray scars fringed both eyes, his nose was spread out across his face like a hawk taking wing, and one of his ears was cauliflower.

With Jerry Bean pushing and Culley pulling, they got Lady Suffolk to her feet. Then the stableman laboriously climbed the ladder to the loft and sent several quarts of oats rattling down the chute to the mare's manger.

She ate the oats with no more appetite than she had the straw, leaving most of them. The two men watched her glumly.

"She's in bad fix," Culley commented.

"That's a fact."

"I paid three hundred dollars for that horse," Culley said.

"That's considerable money," Jerry Bean replied in his soft drawl.

"Considerable," the stable owner agreed. "She must have strained herself. . . . Well, we'll see how she fares in a few days."

During the days and weeks that followed, however, Lady Suffolk showed no improvement. Jerry Bean walked her constantly and groomed her twice a day. He brought her apples and sometimes a lump of sugar and frequently cut up carrots in her oats, but she ate with no interest and never finished a meal. Her ribs and hip bones began to stand out; her head drooped.

"She's still not in good fix," Culley said one morning, a month after he had bought her. "She's off her feed, she's dull in the eye, and her coat is beginning to stare."

"She acts to me like her powder is burned out," Jerry Bean replied.

The old Negro, a man who knew horseflesh, was dead right. In the second half of her race with the clock, Lady Suffolk had been going on borrowed strength, received from the cheers of the crowd, and on pluck, which came only from within her. To finish that terrible contest, she had given the last of the strength and the last of her pluck, suffering an internal hurt in the process. The injury had healed, and the strength was renewable, but not the pluck. As Jerry Bean had put it, her powder was burned out.

Meg Culley, the stable owner's young daughter, came in to see the little gray mare daily, talking to her and petting her. But neither she nor the Negro could bring Lady Suf-

folk out of her demoralized state. There was only one person who could, and he was far away.

"She was a great horse, Jerry Bean," Culley remarked one evening as the two men stood watching Lady Suffolk nose her supper about. "She truly was. If you could have seen her pulling that butcher's wagon! But that race knocked her off her legs for good, I'm persuaded. And she's getting worse every day. I wouldn't have a chance of selling her now. Necessity, it's said, will bring the wolf from the forest. But, as Poor Richard has pointed out, 'Necessity never made a good bargain.'"

"Yes, sir."

"It's clear she cares not whether she lives or dies. I'd be doing her a service by putting a bullet through her head."

"Just wait a bit, Mr. Ford," the Negro urged. "I have a feeling about this little horse."

"I can't afford to wait any longer, Jerry Bean," the stable owner replied. "Not in *this* year of grace. Every one of these nags costs me two bits a day for oats and hay, and I have very little revenue coming in."

"I just have a feeling, Mr. Ford," the Negro told him.

April had passed, and so had May, and they were well into June. That night, for the first time, fireflies appeared in the darkness of the stable. The greenish light, flicking on and off like tiny sparks, made the mare snort nervously.

Later the same night, thunder grumbled in the distance. There was a pause and then it sounded again, louder, closer. The wind began to blow. A Long Island summer storm was coming, and coming fast.

Rain splashed in buckets against the walls and roof of the stable. Lightning flashed, illuminating the interior with a violet glow. It was quickly followed by a splintering crash of thunder that made the bricks under Lady Suffolk's feet vibrate. Then, between the explosions of thunder and the roar of wind and rain, there came another, gentler sound.

Lady Suffolk pricked up her ears. That faint tone was known to her somehow, but from very long ago—and now it was coming from such a great distance.

It sounded again, slightly louder this time. But then lightning flared and thunder boomed, making the mare's ears buzz. She strained to hear above the dashing rain and the roar of the wind, and, once more, the curiously familiar tone sounded.

"Whit-too-wheet!"

The whistle had a tired, sad ring, but it came from a happy time, an old time—springtime with the boy!

Lady Suffolk raised her head and gave a long, joyous neigh. Almost immediately, thunder crashed once more, drowning out her call. She gave it again . . . and again . . . and finally the boy heard, for his answering whistle was sharp and gay.

Minutes later, Stephen Seven Trees was in the stall with Lady Suffolk, his wet face pressed against her cheek, his dripping wet arms around her neck. He had grown taller and he was thin, but he was the boy!

"He had almost given up hope, mighty horse," Stephen told her. "He has been wandering all over New York, New Jersey, and Pennsylvania for the last three years, giving the whistle, and he had almost given up—*almost*."

Then, as in the old days, he chanted to her.

> She's a mighty gray horse
> Oh, she is, yes, she is.

> She's a might gray horse
> That can sleep standing up
> And can trot all day long!

After having been achingly empty for so long, Lady Suffolk felt a strange sensation of fullness. It was love. Outside, the flashing, crashing storm assaulted the stable with a sea of wind-driven rain, but the little gray mare and the boy were snug in the stall.

"Halloo!"

Stephen opened his eyes.

He had been sleeping with his head on Lady Suffolk's warm, massive shoulder. It was the next morning and the storm had passed. The mare had been awake for some time, but she had lain still, so as not to disturb the boy. He jumped to his feet, and she arose, too.

For the first time, he was able to see her pitiful condition, and he gave a gasp of surprise and dismay.

"Who are you?" Meg Culley asked. It was more a demand.

She stood outside the stall with her hands on her hips. She was slender, with long blond hair and golden eyes, and freckles on and around her long, straight nose. She was a girl accustomed to asking questions that were answered, and to giving orders that were obeyed. Some people might have considered her a brat.

"My name is Stephen Seven Trees," the boy replied mildly.

"That's a funny name," she said.

"You like 'Dog' better?" he asked, more sharply. "That's what my uncle used to call me."

"What's wrong with that?" she demanded. "I like dogs."

"I'd rather be called 'Horse,'" he told her.

"What are you doing here?" she asked. "Lo! What's wrong with your eye?"

"Somebody put his fist in it."

"Why?"

"Some people don't like Indians."

"You're an Indian?"

"My father was a Montauk chief."

"I like Indians," Meg said thoughtfully. "Why is your lip split open?"

"Somebody hit me in the mouth."

"Same party that hit you in the eye?"

"Different party."

"You fought them both at the same time?"

"Yes."

"That wasn't very clever of you," she told him.

"The two parties didn't let me decide the matter."

"You haven't answered my question," she pointed out.

"What question, pray? You've asked so many."

"What are you doing in my stable?"

"*Your* stable?"

"Well, it's my father's," she replied. "But what are you doing in it?"

"I've been searching for this horse three years," Stephen said. "And last night I found her."

"How'd you lose her?" Meg shot back.

"I had to go off for a few days, and, when I returned, during the night, I discovered that she was gone—I could see in the moonlight that her stall was empty." Stephen added quickly, to prevent another question, "I looked in

the housekeeper's window. She was gone, too, and everything she owned with her."

"She took Lady Suffolk?"

"No," he replied. "I expect she and my uncle had a
fight—it wouldn't have been their first—and she left. Then
he sold Lady Suffolk to somebody."

"Why didn't you ask your uncle who he had sold Lady
Suffolk to?" Meg asked. She hurriedly corrected herself,
"To whom."

"My uncle and I weren't very close," Stephen answered,
patting the mare's scrawny neck. She laid her head over his
shoulder and rubbed her cheek against his.

"You and Lady Suffolk are, though," Meg observed.
"Reckon you could put her back in good fix?"

"I reckon. How did she get like this?" It was the first
chance he had had to ask the question that was so important
to him.

"Well, I don't know. My father thinks she strained herself just before he bought her. She won't eat and doesn't
seem to have any spirit."

"Trouble? Are you in there?" Ford Culley called.

Meg screwed up her face, pretending to be annoyed at
her father's affectionate nickname. "Papa, come here!" she
ordered. "Look what I found!"

Culley entered the stable, asking, "What is it, Trouble?"

"This is Stephen Six-Something," Meg told her father.

"Stephen Seven Trees," the boy said.

"He's the son of a Montauk chief, and he's been searching for Lady Suffolk for three years, and he's going to put
her back into good fix for you," Meg chattered on.

"Three years," Culley repeated skeptically. "And how

did he support himself all that time?"

"Well, he . . ." Meg turned to the boy. "Stephen, how did you support yourself?"

"In New York and New Jersey, I worked on farms and in livery stables and inns mostly," he told them both. "In Pennsylvania, I did that, too, but I also worked on canal boats and a couple of steamboats. I would feed the hogs or wash dishes or groom horses or just about anything. Then, as soon as I had a couple of dollars, I'd move on, always looking for Lady Suffolk."

Meg nodded, smiling approval at Stephen's frank manner. "That's what he did, Papa," she said.

"How does he know this is the horse he's been seeking?" Culley asked his daughter. "There must be hundreds of gray mares just on Long Island alone."

"Papa, look at the way she acts with him!" Meg exclaimed. "She *has* to be the same horse!"

Pulling on his beard, Culley studied the boy, then remarked, "Appears he was in a disagreement of some kind."

"Two parties that didn't like Indians gave him a thumping," Meg explained. "Papa, we like Indians, don't we."

She was not asking a question. She was telling her father how she expected him to answer.

Meg Culley ruled the Culley roost. Her mother was frequently a rebel, but her father seldom challenged his daughter's authority.

"Yes, Trouble, we like Indians," Culley replied uncertainly.

"Then he can stay and put Lady Suffolk back into good fix and tell me all about Indians!" the girl exclaimed.

Sadly, her father shook his head.

"I'm sorry, Meg," he told her, "but I just can't afford to take in anybody else—not in these times."

"Sir, I could sleep in the loft," Stephen told Culley. "I'll eat whatever is left over after everyone else eats. If there's nothing left over, I won't eat."

"Appears to me he could do with some vittles right now," Meg remarked to Lady Suffolk.

"Well, I expect we could give you breakfast," Culley told the boy. "But then you'll have to be on your way. I'd like to let you stay with all my heart, but I cannot. Poor Richard says, 'Three good meals a day is bad living,' and yet a body has to eat to live and I simply cannot afford another mouth to feed in this year of grace."

"Papa," Meg told him firmly, "Stephen will put Lady Suffolk back into good fix."

She turned to the boy. "Why don't you go up into the loft and send down some breakfast to her and see if she'll eat?"

Stephen glanced at the girl's father, who nodded, although his face showed his annoyance. The boy climbed the ladder to the loft and, shortly afterward, the oats came rattling down the chute into the little gray mare's manger.

She ignored them until the boy came back down the ladder and told her, "Eat 'em up, Lady Suffolk. Eat 'em up!"

Meg, her father, Stephen, and Jerry Bean, who had just come out of his room, stood around the stall, watching the mare eat as she hadn't eaten in months.

"Papa?" Meg asked.

"Very well, Trouble," Culley replied. "He can stay."

After that, Meg Culley spent most of each day watching Stephen work with Lady Suffolk and help Jerry Bean with the other horses.

"Lo! What's that?" she asked the boy one morning as he was rubbing the mare's legs with some liquid.

"Liniment."

"What's it do?"

"Takes away aches and pains."

"What's it made of?"

"White oak bark soaked in boiling water."

"Is that Indian medicine?"

"Montauk Indian medicine."

"Hmm!"

Meg, who had been making inquiries as soon as she could talk, was fascinated with Indian life and customs. She never tired of listening to Stephen, and he enjoyed answering her endless questions—most of the time.

"What's the Montauk word for white man?" she asked after supper one evening.

"*Wonnux.*"

"What am I?"

"*Squashees.*"

"What's that mean?"

"Little girl."

"Little girl! I'm twelve years old! How old are you?"

"Fourteen," he replied proudly.

"Well, I'm still a young woman. What's the Montauk for that?"

"*Yunks quash.*"

"I'd rather be a *yunks quash* than—whatever you called it. Stephen, you said your father was a chief?"

"Yes, a Grand Sachem. He was chief of *all* the Montauks."

"What was his name?"

A stiffness came over the boy's face and he dropped his eyes. "I can't tell you."

"Very well, Stephen," she replied primly, getting up to leave. "I expect it's none of my business."

"It's bad luck to speak the names of the dead out loud," he told her quietly.

"Do you really believe that?" she asked—not scornful, just interested.

"I sure do. I spoke the names of my father and mother just before I left to go on my spirit dream, and that's how I lost Lady Suffolk."

"Yes, but Stephen, don't you think it might have just happened . . . spirit dream!"

"Margaret Elizabeth!" her mother called from the house.

"I'll be in soon, Mama!" Meg answered.

She turned back to the boy, hugging herself as a thrill went through her. "Now then, Stephen, what's a spirit dream, and what was *your* spirit dream?"

Leaning forward, he said softly, "I'll tell you."

13

THE SPIRIT DREAM

"Well, tell me, Stephen!" Meg demanded impatiently.

"I'm trying to think how to begin," Stephen Seven Trees replied uncertainly, gazing at Lady Suffolk as though for inspiration.

"At the beginning, Stephen, at the beginning!"

"Every Montauk boy, when he's about eleven or twelve years old, must be ready to have his spirit dream," Stephen told her. "When the *Manitos* call him, he paints his face black and goes into the woods—"

"Stephen," Meg broke in, "what are *Manitos*?"

"Our gods. We have many—spirits of the north, south, east, and west, and the winds that blow from them, spirits of the sea and the sky, the sun and the rain, night and day."

"How do they call you?"

"They enter into our thoughts and tell us the time has come for us to go out and have our spirit dream."

"Why do you paint your face black?"

"Because that is what a Montauk boy does when he sets

out to have a spirit dream. But if you keep interrupting," he pointed out mildly, "I can't tell you the dream."

"I'm sorry, Stephen, it's all so interesting."

Lady Suffolk saw Jerry Bean come out of his room, carrying his supper dishes in his gnarled black hands.

"Everybody so serious," he drawled casually as he made his way past the boy and girl. "Y'all act like you're fixing to overthrow the government."

Meg looked at Stephen.

"I didn't mean to interrupt," the old Negro said rather stiffly, continuing on his way. "Y'all go right ahead."

"I was just telling Meg about my spirit dream," Stephen told him. "You're welcome to listen, too."

The Negro stopped and turned. "I've heard of them," he said.

"They're not secret," Stephen remarked to Meg. "Whenever a Montauk boy had his, he told it like a story, sitting around the fire. Sometimes he chanted it."

"Go ahead." Then she added, "Without the chanting, please."

"The boy would go into the woods and fast, waiting to have his spirit dream and watching for his spirit guide."

Before Meg could ask, he explained, "This might be a bird or an animal or a person. Whatever it was, the boy would know that it would help him for the rest of his life."

"My!" Meg breathed.

"I went into the woods and climbed a hill," Stephen told them. "At the top, I put a pinch of herbs at each of the four points of the compass. This was to show that I wished to receive messages from the four directions of the winds and was waiting for my spirit guide. I fasted for three days, and then, that night, the spirit dream came to me."

"Oh, my!" Meg exclaimed, hugging herself. Then she promptly slapped a hand over her mouth.

"I was all alone in a great, gray fog. It was as though I was the only person on earth. The fog came along in tall drifts, like the ghosts of all my ancestors marching by, and then I heard a sound from far away. It kept getting louder, and, finally, I could make out what it was."

"Well, what was it?" Meg demanded.

"It was the sound of hoofbeats and the rumble of wheels. At last, a gray horse appeared out of the fog. It was as though the fog had closed in to make her. She was pulling an empty wagon."

Meg clapped her hands, exclaiming, "Your spirit guide is Lady Suffolk!"

Stephen nodded. "My spirit guide is Lady Suffolk. I climbed into the wagon and drove," he went on. "The fog had changed to pitch darkness, with hard rain. We started to go faster and faster. I heard other horses and wagons on each side of me. There was a loud roaring.

"Then lightning flashed and I could see for miles. The roaring sound was from a huge crowd of people, cheering. Then there was a fireplace in the road ahead. A boy was working a bellows, fanning the flames. Suddenly, there were two boys. The fireplace got bigger and bigger until it became a brick gate and we drove in. One boy jumped into the wagon and we started to fight."

"Oh, my!" Meg exclaimed, and slap went that hand over her mouth.

"I threw him out," Stephen went on. "Then his friend jumped in and *we* started to fight."

"Do tell!"

Spank that mouth as often as she did, Meg Culley just couldn't keep it still. The expression she had used reminded Stephen of his uncle's housekeeper, Mrs. Eller, and he thought of her fondly, wondering what had happened to her.

"It's considered fair for two boys to fight one," Jerry Bean told Stephen. "It's called 'One Down and the Other Come On.' The two are never at the other boy both at once, but, as soon as one is knocked down or thrown, the other can rush in and continue the battle."

"Is that the game you were playing with those two parties just before you came here?" Meg asked.

"I expect those two parties never heard of that game," Stephen replied dryly.

Meg slapped her mouth with such authority that she made the little gray mare jump.

"I gave the second boy a good one and he disappeared," Stephen said. Then my vision song came to me." He sang,

> Like a hawk I fly.
> Like a whale I swim.
> Into the wind—
> Against the waves—
> I go my way!

"Doesn't rhyme," Meg remarked.

Stephen told her quietly, "Vision songs are not supposed to rhyme."

"I'm sorry," she replied. "It's a lovely song, Stephen."

"Thank you," the boy said shyly, then continued describing his dream. "The fire in the fireplace had turned into a burning forest and we were driving through it, with blazing trees falling all around us. Then we came to a scarecrow with long arms and white gloves, standing beside the road. As we passed him, he swung around, knocking me out of the wagon.

"I ran after the wagon, but my feet seemed to be in tar and I couldn't catch up with it. Suddenly, flights of black arrows flew out from the wheels, and the horse and wagon disappeared down the road, and then all I could hear were the hoofbeats and the rumble of wheels."

"And then?" Meg asked.

"That's all."

"My! What does it all mean, do you reckon?"

"I expect it's a jumble of things that have already happened and maybe are going to happen," he replied. "I wish there was somebody who could explain it to me. In our village, we had a *powwas*, witch doctor, who could tell what dreams and visions meant, but I remember he died in the plague—after he had dreamed his own death."

"My!" Meg shot him a skeptical glance.

Stephen paid no attention, talking almost to himself, "Well, I've spent three years searching for this horse, and now that I've found her, no one will ever take her away from me again." He reached into her stall and patted the little gray mare, who gave him back a joyous neigh.

"Margaret Elizabeth!" her mother called. "You come in at once!"

Meg collected the supper dishes and said good night.

Stephen Seven Trees's presence alone made the pluck flow back into Lady Suffolk, as the moon causes the flooding tide. Moreover, his constant grooming, along with the nourishing and plentiful food, which she now ate with an appetite, began to put her back into good fix.

One warm afternoon, when the pair came pounding up to the livery stable after a long ride along the back roads, Jerry Bean was standing in the doorway, waiting.

"Y'all work right well together," he remarked. "You know how to handle a horse, Stephen. How are you with your fists?"

The boy leaped off the mare and brought her to the trough. He said, "I can wrestle."

"You don't know anything about milling?"

"My uncle taught me how to fall," Stephen replied dryly.

"Would you be interested in learning how to mill?"

"I would, yes."

"I do believe the notion is a good one," the old Negro said. "We can start the lesson as soon as you finish with Lady Suffolk."

Working in circles, moving from her head back, Stephen ran a comb through the little gray mare's coat, which had regained its smooth, glossy texture. Then he gave her a thorough brushing, softly chanting his vision song.

> Like a hawk I fly.
> Like a whale I swim.
> Into the wind—
> Against the waves—
> I go my way!

After he had fed the mare, he went out of the stable. She watched, chewing her oats.

Jerry Bean was waiting for him in the yard. So was Meg Culley.

"Oh, no!" Stephen said with unusual firmness. "No spectators—'specially girls!"

"Stephen, this is my . . ." Meg began.

Then she hushed as if she had clapped a hand over her mouth. Stalking into the stable, she went over to Lady Suffolk's stall.

"Boys are stupid," she told the little gray mare. " 'Specially Indian boys!"

Lady Suffolk went on crunching her oats.

"Now I'll tell you what it is about milling," Jerry Bean said to Stephen, out in the yard. "The wise boxer uses *these*—" he held up his big, black fists—"and *these*—" he pointed to his feet—"and *this*—" and he held a finger to his temple.

"A milling match, Stephen, is not a wrestling match—even though you will see many fighters in the prize ring today grappling with each other like a couple of schoolboys. It's 40 to 50 per cent in favor of the boxer over the wrestler. I've paid dear enough for that opinion, and it's mine. With me so far?"

"I am."

"You've seen the way Lady Suffolk trots," the Negro went on. "The wise boxer is just as fancy a stepper. In and out—*in*, blocking your man's blows, getting to him with short, quick jabs and chops—and *out* before he can recover himself."

As he spoke, Jerry Bean assumed a boxer's stance—left arm extended almost its full length, right cocked like the hammer of a pistol. For a few seconds, the heavy years seemed to fall away as he straightened up and quickly moved forward on legs that had momentarily lost their stiffness, swinging his fists, then pulling back. Stephen watched as though seeing a vision.

"You must be a famous fighter," he said.

"No, not famous," the old Negro replied with a rueful smile, "although I would give odds that the name of Jumping Jerry Bean is still remembered in some quarters of the republic. But, Stephen, I came up to the scratch too many times, over too many years. I couldn't move as fast as before, and that's when I began to collect *this*—" he pointed to his cauliflower ear—"and *this*—" he indicated his nose— "and *these*—" and he held a finger to his scarred eyes. "Now then, you try it."

Every evening after that, when they had finished their chores, Stephen and Jerry Bean worked on the boy's milling. Lady Suffolk watched from her stall as the old boxer had Stephen jump forward and backward over logs, to develop the spring in his legs, and taught him the art of getting inside the defense of his opponent and dealing him short, quick blows.

Lady Suffolk was not the only spectator to the workouts. Almost every evening, Meg Culley would crawl under a rhododendron bush at the end of the stable, watching the forbidden lessons with a sly smile, occasionally chuckling to herself and murmuring, "No spectators—'specially girls!"

Meanwhile, Stephen was making such progress with Lady Suffolk that Meg's father began to use her as his personal roadster. Sundays, she took the Culley family to church in the buggy.

Going to and from the services, it was the custom of the cracks to let their horses out in a bit of informal racing, or "brushing." Ford Culley entered into this practice with a will, to the disapproval of his wife, and the delight of his daughter.

A common sight Sundays was a little gray mare going down the road in a flying trot. She was pulling a buggy in which sat a bearded man, a woman, and a girl, all wearing their Sunday best. The features of the man and girl were bright and eager, while the prim-faced woman sitting beside them seemed to be trying to hide under her parasol as the gray mare gaily took them past one vehicle after another.

One Sunday in deep summer, when they drew up at the white frame chapel after a particularly successful drive, Mary Culley turned to her husband.

"Ford, you are making a fool of yourself!" she snapped.

"Fool am I?" he replied, still flushed from his last victory. "I rode faster behind this little mare just now than ever I rode in my life!"

"That is exactly what I am talking about," she went on in her precise way. "You are a grown man—not in the best of health, I might add—and you are racing boys less than half your age."

"Mary, brushing isn't racing," Culley told her. "It's . . . well, it's just brushing."

"You're making a fool of yourself, and those boys are laughing at you."

"Laughing are they? *Laughing* are they? Well, I'll make the honorable gentlemen sing out a little more on the other side of their mouths!"

[145]

"Mama, Papa, we'll be late for the service," Meg told them.

Uncommon for her, she permitted her father to help her to the ground. Mrs. Culley, on her part, refused his aid— and almost fell as a result. He hitched Lady Suffolk to the rail, where horses in harness and under saddle were tethered. The Culleys then joined the stream of Christians flowing toward the chapel and its pastor, who stood on the steps, Bible in his left hand, right hand outstretched to greet the members of his flock and draw them inside.

The day was hot, with white clouds like the sails of an armada passing across the blue, and Lady Suffolk felt drowsy. The singing came to her in waves.

> Rock of Ages, cleft for me.
> Let me hide myself in Thee. . . .
> Be of sin the double cure,
> Cleanse me from its guilt and power. . . .

She, and most of the other horses with her, dozed. The thunderous voice of Parson Oates awoke her with a start.

"Babylon! That's what we have in our midst, Babylon! I say unto you, only fast people keep fast horses! Such horseflesh is an ally of the Father of Evil! Racing is sinful. Racing is profane. . . ."

Once more, Lady Suffolk dozed. She did not wake up until Ford Culley untied her, when the flock came streaming out of the chapel and toward the line of horses. Mary Culley nodded, smiling, to a young couple, then snapped at her husband, "I hope you took that sermon to heart."

"As Poor Richard has put it so well, 'A good Example is the best Sermon,' " Culley replied. "I have seen on more than one occasion the good Parson let his nag out considerable when he was late for an appointment—like a free meal, I expect. Go ahead, Lady Suffolk!"

Mary Culley smiled at another couple and said out of the side of her mouth, "But he wasn't *racing*, Ford."

"My dear," her husband replied evenly, "when a horse races, he is going as fast as he can, correct? A trotter could go faster by breaking into a gallop, correct? Ergo, a trotter is not racing."

"Oh, go to Jericho with you! You're horse crazy. You've got Fetlock Fever!"

"It's not fatal."

"Ford, if a trotter could go faster, what is so almighty fine about trotting?"

"My dear, through his rhythm, smoothness and precision, through the perfect release of his powers, by that vital quality in him called 'the trotting instinct,' the trotter transmutes the raw material of speed into a work of art, just as the alchemist transforms base metal into gold."

"Papa," Meg said, "party coming up fast on your left."

"Oh, for mercy's sake!" her mother exclaimed.

Culley waited until the other vehicle, with its single occupant, was even with him. Then he gave Lady Suffolk the word, and away they went.

14

A RACE WITH
AN IRON HORSE

Jerry Bean and Stephen Seven Trees had just finished watering the horses next morning when Ford Culley and two other men entered the stable.

"Dark Hollow Ranch," Culley remarked. "That would be five and twenty miles round trip. If you're going to catch the afternoon train back to the City, you'll need a stepper. I could give you John Paul Jones there, but he's a mite gimpy in the forefoot. Frigate would take you there in fine order, but as for the return trip— Poor Richard has said, 'Time is money.' I expect the horse for you is Lady Suffolk here. Her great-grandsire was Messenger, and I believe you'll find there's considerable trot in those little gray legs."

"Messenger, eh?" the taller of the two men asked with interest. He studied the gray mare closely.

"George!" he exclaimed to his companion. "Look at that front! Mark those quarters!"

"I don't know that I've ever seen such muscular development in a horse this size," George replied. "Incredible!"

Culley began to swell with pride.

"The butcher I bought her from claimed she was all whalebone and wire," he told them.

"She was a butcher's horse!" the first man said. "That explains it. For a horse to pull a meat wagon is the same as for a man to be a galley slave. If they can just live through the experience, they're the strongest creatures for their size there is."

The two men climbed into the buggy, with George in the driver's seat.

"Now for it, Lady Suffolk," he told her. "Let's see your way of going."

The day was fine, the road smooth, the little gray mare in the best of spirits. Her passengers, sports journalists from New York City, sat back and enjoyed the ride, quietly discussing their work.

Then George exclaimed, "Tim, will you look at this little mare? One ear cocked forward, the other back—she's not missing a thing!"

"The livery man said she was a stepper, and that she is," Tim replied. "It's plain to see she enjoys a workout."

Upon their arrival at Dark Hollow Ranch, the journalists left Lady Suffolk with one of the hands and went about their business. The hand watered, fed, and groomed her, then left her tethered in the cool shade of an oak tree, thoroughly enjoying the breeze. When the journalists came back from dinner, she was well rested and raring to go.

She clip-clopped down the road in the bright July sunlight, clipping off the distance home. The road passed a long brown pond, spotted with lily pads. Snapping turtles, like muddy green helmets on the mossy logs, paid her no attention. But, as she raced past, bullfrogs by the dozens leaped into the water with the twang of snapped bowstrings.

A puffing roar sounded, and, presently, a big black locomotive appeared on the left, pulling a string of cars. For about a mile, the road and the tracks ran parallel. The little gray mare and the iron horse pounded along side by side.

"Go ahead, Lady Suffolk!" George urged.

She began to trot faster . . . and ever faster. Aboard the engine, the fireman started to hurl logs into the blazing firebox. Thick, creamy smoke gushed from the locomotive's stack and great masses of vapor hissed from its pistons, as white as the clouds overhead in the sunlight. The engineer was shouting to the fireman and frantically ringing his bell, as if this would somehow get more speed out of the locomotive.

"Go ahead, Lady Suffolk!"

She sensed rather than heard the appeal, for the engine was making a terrible racket. Passengers in the rocking, clattering, banging cars stared in open-mouthed amazement, yanking on each other's arms and pointing as, clop by clop, the little gray mare pulled in front of the iron horse.

Up ahead was a deep forest, a wall of flickering green in the breezy sunlight. Lady Suffolk, trotting like she had never trotted before, held her lead right up to the edge of the forest and even increased it by a couple of lengths. Then, almost at once, several things happened.

A cloud passed over the sun. The forest was gloomy dark. In the poor light, the sparks from the smokestack—invisible

in the sunshine—were vividly clear. Wind beat a furnace blast of air against Lady Suffolk. She was surrounded by choking smoke, in a swirling blizzard of sparks that bit her like a swarm of horseflies.

Panic-stricken, she lost the rhythm of her stroke and broke her stride. A foot flew up and the shoe slashed her on the belly. The locomotive roared on, pulling one rocking, clattering, banging car after another past her, but, in her panic, she was blind to them and their gawking passengers.

Her driver, an experienced reinsman, did not use the whip. Instead, he pulled her head slightly to one side, away from the train, then upward, in a quick, firm but not violent movement. Almost at once, she collected herself and resumed her trot.

There was no catching the locomotive, however. Superhorse Lady Suffolk was without question. Supernatural she was not, despite the many legends about her to the contrary, such as the one that grew up from her race with the iron horse. For hundreds of people had witnessed her deed, and it grew in their imaginations and in the mouths of others they told it to, until it reached the proportions of a myth.

Lady Suffolk was still flesh and blood. Fine as that flesh was, it nonetheless became tired eventually, and there was a point where that rich blood could not hustle fast enough to bring it oxygen and energy. For a short time, the little gray mare had held her own—more than held her own—with an iron horse, but the time had passed.

Anyhow, on the other side of the forest, the tracks curved off to the left and the road went to the right, so the race could not be continued.

"Incredible!" George exclaimed when he had gathered his wits together.

"Her work speaks for itself, trumpet-tongued," his companion told him. "If that liveryman doesn't make a race mare out of her, he's a tomfool."

"Incredible!"

The two journalists could talk about nothing else but Lady Suffolk and her feat during the rest of the journey. One ear cocked forward, the other back, the little gray mare never missed a thing.

She was thoroughly blown and covered with lather when she finally drew up at the livery stable, but she was still in the best of spirits, and the boy was waiting. He threw a blanket over her and began to water her out.

The two journalists were talking to Ford Culley, who was swelling with pride at their words.

"If she settles into a handy style of going—one that wastes none of her power in false movement—she can beat them all," Tim said.

"The chances of Lady Suffolk reaching the top of the tree are as good as those of any horse out," George told Culley. "She has all the elements—high breeding, capital action, immense speed, indomitable game and thorough bottom.

The stable owner shook his head, laughing gaily.

"Please, gentlemen," he said, "don't set me down for a croaker, but a little brushing with the nags hereabouts is one thing, and trying conclusions with the top horseflesh in the republic is something else entirely. She is, after all, a small horse."

"Not in her moving parts, she isn't," Tim told him. "The

notion that a big, bulky horse will make a fast trotter is plain wrong. And I don't reckon that a tall horse would have any advantage over this mare. The tall horse is apt to be leggy, and his height often comes from the extra length in the cannon bones, which gives no power.''

"I know," Culley replied, "but—"

"Length in the arms, shoulders, thighs and haunches—such as she has—is a different matter altogether," Tim broke in. "I pay no mind to those who insist that a trotter should be straight in the shoulder and short in the carcass. The best ones I've known weren't punched up, but the reverse, like this mare.''

'Well, don't set me down for a croaker. . . .''

"Mr. Culley," Tim said, "I've been a rail bird for five and thirty years, and I've never once seen a trotter that had Lady Suffolk's potential. With the proper training, there's no horse she couldn't show her heels to.''

"Pistol?" Culley asked. "With Leonard Toms up?"

"Aye.''

"Front Street, with Madison Wiles?"

"Aye.''

"Well, I don't know.''

"If you'd seen what George and I saw today, you'd know.''

"Incredible!" George exclaimed.

"Ever since Sally Miller took a sulky over the Hunting Park Course in two minutes and thirty-seven seconds, in 1834, horse trainers have been trying to develop a trotting machine that could break the two-and-a-half-minute mile," Tim said. Then, like a judge handing down a decision, he

solemnly declared, "It is my opinion that in Lady Suffolk
you have that machine."

"Yes, sir?" Culley asked.

"Yes, sir!"

"Yes, sir!" George added.

The liveryman chuckled. He was so full of pride that
his shirt felt too tight. This had to be one of the best days
in his life. "Well, don't set me down for a croaker. . . ."

By the time Stephen had finished watering Lady Suffolk
out, the two journalists had left to catch their train. The
boy gave the mare a bath with soap and hot water. The
strong lye soap made the cut on her belly burn, but she
stood quietly. Stephen rinsed her with cool water, rubbed
her with towels, and walked her until she was dry.

Then he brought her back to her stall, climbed the ladder to the loft, and returned with his wolf pelt. Untying it,
he took out a jar of bear grease and rubbed some on the
cut. The smell brought back the old fear, but, in the boy's
hands, she was confident, and the grease soothed the
burning.

"Lo, what's this?" Meg asked, coming up.

"Wolf pelt," Stephen replied.

"Did you kill the wolf?" she asked quickly.

"No."

"Anyway, I wasn't talking about that," she said. "I meant
this belt of beads."

"Wampum."

"What's it for?"

"It's a message."

"What's it say?"

Meg Culley threw questions the way some men threw

fists. With Meg, Stephen couldn't duck or dodge or leap back as Jerry Bean had taught him to do. She was too quick, too insistent. And yet he did not resent her curiosity, for he was fully aware of her fascination with Indian life and customs.

"I expect you'd call it a deed to some property," Stephen replied.

Meg studied the figures in the wampum. Then, pointing to one, she exclaimed, "That's you!"

"Correct," he replied with a smile. "How did you know?"

"It's a pine tree with six beads around it. Six and one is seven. Stephen Seven Trees!"

"Correct." His smile broadened.

"I don't know what that thing on the end is," she said, "but *this* looks like a flower and *these* look like animal tracks, and that thing at the beginning looks like a man sitting down with his hands up."

"You're very good," Stephen told her with great admiration. "That's exactly what the first figure is—it's the sign for Storyteller, the Keeper of the Wampum."

"Oh!" Meg gasped, hugging herself.

Pointing from one figure to the next, Stephen read, "To Storyteller from Wolf Bear and Heather Blossom—our son, Stephen Seven Trees, inherits from us the plot of ground known as the Bee's Nest."

"Does this show where the Bee's Nest is?" Meg pointed to the doeskin map.

"Yes."

"Hmm." She was silent for a moment . . . but only for a moment. Then she asked "Storyteller didn't die from the smallpox?"

"No, he lives in another village. And he has a belt just like this one that my father had made for him at the same time he had this one made for me."

"That last figure is supposed to be a bee?"

"Correct."

"Why is there a line around it?"

"To show I inherit the whole piece of ground. My father took me to the Bee's Nest when I was a little boy," Stephen went on. "It's called that because it has so many wild flowers. It's on a cliff that overlooks the sea. It's really a beautiful place. I'd like you to see it. . . ."

"Stephen, what's the matter?" Meg was staring at him in astonishment.

The boy asked in a quivering voice, "Did I tell you the names of my parents?"

"Oh, that's right!" she exclaimed.

Stephen put his arms around Lady Suffolk's neck, trying to borrow some of her pluck.

"Something bad is going to happen, just like it did the last time I spoke their names," he said grimly. "Maybe my uncle will come."

"But why?" Meg asked. "Would he try to steal the wampum?"

"That wouldn't do him any good," the boy replied. "The Bee's Nest is mine, as the wampum says. But after I took it over, if he had control over me, he could sell the land, piece by piece, and he'd be rich."

"So if he comes around . . ." Meg began.

"He'll be after *me*," Stephen went on. "If you ever see a man as tall as a pine tree, with a pair of eyes that peer out at you like wild animals from their caves, would you let me know?''

"I certainly will," she answered, anxious to calm him down.

"He always dresses in black, and he is *never* without his white silk gloves."

"White gloves," Meg remarked thoughtfully. "Stephen, he's the scarecrow in your spirit dream!"

"That's right. I hadn't thought of that. Well, he'll never take me away from Lady Suffolk, or her away from me. He'll have to kill me first!"

15

TO THE BEACON

Two mornings later, Stephen and Jerry Bean were watering the horses when Ford Culley drove Frigate up to the stableyard. He was sitting behind her in a strange vehicle. It had two huge wheels, with long, slender, black spokes, and a single seat.

Mary Culley and her daughter, who had come out on the back porch after doing the breakfast dishes, to enjoy the morning breeze, walked over to the new contraption. Meg was smiling. Her mother was not.

"And what do you call that?" Mary Culley asked.

"Well, now, I call it a sulky, since that's what it is," her husband replied. "It's what the whips of the turf use."

"Oh, and now we're a whip of the turf," Mrs. Culley commented.

"I don't know about you, my dear. I reckoned I might try my hand."

Annoyance stiffened her face.

"I know," the liveryman replied sympathetically. "Pretty

[161]

loud smell of axle grease here. But it makes these wheels hum a clever tune, and that's a fact."

He jumped not too heavily to the ground.

"She's a beauty, ain't she?" he asked. "Shafts of American ash. The axle well-tempered iron, four feet even from linchpin to linchpin. And she weighs no more than eight and fifty pounds!"

From the expression on his wife's face, Culley might have been talking about some female rival of hers.

"Mark those wheels, my dear! Have you ever seen such beauty, such grace? But notice the size of them. We know now that only big wheels will ever crack the two-and-a-half-minute mile, and these fine fellows are five feet in diameter!"

"Oh, for mercy's sake!" Mary Culley exploded. "Yesterday, you were a happy husband and father. Today, you're a whip on the turf. Tomorrow, you're going to crack the two-and-a-half-minute mile!"

"Perhaps today, my dear."

"Today!"

Lady Suffolk started at her tone. Meg Culley clapped a hand over her mouth. Stephen and Jerry Bean exchanged concerned glances.

"I thought I'd drive Lady Suffolk over to the Beacon Course and try conclusions with some of the nags there this afternoon."

"Where's the Beacon Course?" Mrs. Culley asked.

"New Jersey," her husband replied casually.

"New Jersey!" Mary Culley and her daughter screamed together, and Lady Suffolk gave a nervous neigh as Stephen and Jerry Bean exchanged glances considerably more concerned than before. New Jersey!

"Oh, it's not too far," Culley remarked. "Most of the journey is on the Brooklyn ferry. We'll be back by dark, I expect."

"Ford, if you have no concern about driving that poor mare all day, think about yourself," his wife urged.

Culley snorted. "I'm as strong as a horse."

"Not that horse," Mrs. Culley snapped. "Nor any horse." She leaned toward him, her voice low and urgent. "Ford, listen to me. If you *must* race the mare, let Stephen drive her!"

Now the boy and Meg exchanged a look.

"As Poor Richard has put it so well," Culley replied, " 'He that by the plow would thrive, himself must either hold or drive.' "

"You're not behind a plow, *old* man," his wife told him. "Ford, please, Meg and I would like to have you with us for a time. I declare, ever since that little gray horse came into your life, you've been acting like an eighteen-year-old boy, and your health won't stand it!"

"My health, thank you kindly, is perfect," Culley replied. "As Poor Richard says, 'Early to bed and early to rise—"

"Poor Richard, Poor Richard, Poor Richard! I wish to heaven you had never laid your hands on that book! I do believe it's the only one you've ever read. You keep repeating those stupid sayings as though they were Scripture, or some kind of Mumbo Jumbo. Like 'Tippecanoe and Tyler, too.' But not *you*!"

Hiding her angry tears, Mary Culley stormed out of the

stableyard, retreating to the sanctuary of her kitchen, locking and bolting the door behind her.

" 'Whatever's begun in anger, ends in shame,' " the liveryman quoted softly to the handle of his whip. "Well, be it so. 'Time is money,' and we must be on our way. Jerry Bean, Stephen, would you kindly oblige me by unhitching Frigate, one of you, while the other hitches Lady Suffolk to the sulky? Meg, wish your father luck."

"Good luck, Papa."

" 'Diligence is the mother of good luck,' " he quoted.

When Lady Suffolk was in the shafts of the sulky, the Negro stepped forward politely.

"She's all there, Mr. Ford," he said in his soft, liquid voice. "Stephen has put her in the top of her form for you. I'm certainly not trying to tell you how to race her, but you know that the right kind of touch and movement in the reins and bit is worth more than all the whipping in the world."

"Thank you, Jerry Bean," Culley replied. "But also don't forget Poor Richard's maxim, 'The things which hurt, instruct.' I'm off. Farewell, all of you!"

"Jerry Bean, Stephen," he called as he drove away, "look after the stable while I'm gone. Remember, 'A little neglect may breed mischief; for want of a nail the shoe was lost; for want of a shoe the horse was lost; and for want of a horse the rider was lost!' "

Stephen stared up at his friend's battered black face.

"Jerry Bean," he asked, "what's the matter?"

The old Negro shrugged his heavy shoulders. "Mr. Ford is too wise to take counsel from a former slave."

* * *

"Go ahead, Lady Suffolk! Go ahead!"

The morning was cool for the end of July, and the little gray mare was in excellent form. With Culley's encouragement, she began to step out. By the time they reached the outskirts of Brooklyn, they had engaged in three brushes and from all three had emerged triumphant.

Both horse and driver were tired, although not too tired. The little gray mare would cheerfully have brushed several more times before making the return trip. She had no way of knowing that her resolute master had not yet begun to race.

The hubbub and hullabaloo of downtown Brooklyn, however, quickly revived them both. They joined a stream of wagons, carts, and vans, rumbling over the bricks toward the river, while another stream of wagons, carts, and vans came rumbling at them on the other side of the thoroughfare. Meanwhile, in the gutters on both sides of the street, crowds of highly vocal hogs searched for a second breakfast, or an early lunch.

As Lady Suffolk drew near the water, the bricks became wet and slippery, and the squatty brown and gray buildings ahead were dim in the swirling white mists. The ferry, a small sidewheeler with two tall, black smokestacks, was riding up and down in the waves, grinding and thumping against the splintered timbers of the pier as if anxious to be off.

The ferry captain, a round-faced, round-bodied, elderly man, stood outside the wheel house on the hurricane deck, with legs wide-spread. He was shouting commands, weather comments and predictions, and remarks in a voice that sounded as though he had met and faced down many a shrieking hurricane from this little deck.

The ferry was small enough for everyone coming aboard or already on board to hear him clearly if he just raised that fearsome voice one octave. But he used a speaking trumpet in addition, roaring out the clipped sentences like cannon shots.

"Stand by to cast off bow lines! Stand by to cast off stern lines! Never seen it so raw for July! An early frost, I fear! Come along, sir! (This to Culley, who was in the process of driving Lady Suffolk down the gangplank onto the lower deck of the ferry.) Soon as her groceries are stowed, the *Empire State* is off like a rocket! Stand by to get under way!" (This last explosion was directed at the helmsman in the wheel house, three feet away.)

Presently, following similar trumpet blasts, a bell rang, a whistle tooted, and the deck under Lady Suffolk's feet trembled as the two paddle wheels began to whirl, thrashing the brown water until it foamed white. The *Empire State* was off; if not like a rocket, she was at least under way.

The pitch and roll of the little vessel, although not severe, was enough to keep Lady Suffolk and the other horses aboard off-balance and snorting nervously.

The fog soon blocked out Brooklyn. Ahead was nothing but more swirling whiteness, so that the ferry seemed to be in the middle of a cloud. Bells rang and whistles tooted as other ferries, like mammoth water bugs, went splashing past.

The *Empire State* clawed her way up the Hudson River, fighting the strong current.

At last, Lady Suffolk sniffed the air and gave a relieved neigh. Grass. Land. Solid ground. The other horses picked up the cry. Shortly, the flapping of sails and the flutter of flags came to the little gray mare's ears, and, soon after that, a thicket of masts loomed out of the fog ahead.

In answer to blasts from the speaking trumpet, bow and stern lines leaped out and over the piles on the pier like lassos. Then the ferry crew manned the clinking capstans, warping the vessel against the pier. At last, Lady Suffolk clomped up the gangplank onto the land, wobble-legged and a bit dizzy, but glad to be back on solid ground.

It was by then early afternoon. The summer sun had begun to burn off the fog, shining down upon the line of omnibuses, coaches, cabs, and carriages streaming toward the race course. It shone down with equal radiance upon the carts and wagons, and the thousands of people going on shanks' mare. Picnic baskets were clamped to the arms of many of the women, and everyone was in a holiday mood.

The Beacon Course was on the western slope of the Jersey City Heights, overlooking the broad green grassland of the Newark Meadows.

When Lady Suffolk and her master entered the course, the stands were packed; the entire inside of the track was lined with carriages; and the balcony of the clubhouse was filled with women. Their silks and satins were flashing in the sunlight, their ribbons and tassels fluttering in the breeze. As much as the bright colors dazzled and annoyed the little gray mare, they were a feast for the eyes of Ford Culley.

The mare and her master passed a man in a straw hat, with his face painted black, hopping about like a crow on a tiny platform, furiously plunking a banjo. Also on the platform was a tin cup into which people occasionally dropped coppers—*occasionally.*

Horse and driver passed a white-bearded man with a forehead like a boulder, who stood outside a tent, pointing his cane at a diagram of the human skull.

"Here above the eye, my friends, is the seat of logic. Here on the top of the head can be found firmness, and here, high over the ear, is caution. Each and every trait of your personality, my friends, is shown by the size and shape of the bumps on your head. Why be ignorant when Dr. Cestus can tell you all? Step inside and the celebrated Dr. Cestus will read your head for you, for just two bits a head!"

Further on, the pair came to a crowd gathered before a wooden stand on which rested a barrel. A man stood in front of it, doggedly cranking a hurdy-gurdy.

> Hail Columbia! Happy land!
> Hail, ye heroes! Heaven-born band. . . .

When the anthem had wheezed to a close, the cranker withdrew and another man stepped up.

He was tall and thin as a rake handle, with a clean-shaven hatchet face that looked as though it had been exposed to large weighty volumes far more than to the sun. His stooped posture and big rectangular spectacles, over which he peered benignly at the crowd, gave him the air of a scholar. Yet he wore a faded blue hunting shirt and patched woolen trousers, held up by suspenders, the costume of a typical "stagecoach lawyer."

He filled a mug from the barrel and held it out to the crowd. A hand quickly accepted it, and the pale man filled another mug, which vanished just as quickly.

The speaker was an educated man from the upper class, but he assumed home spun dress and speech to win voters to the Whig ticket. "It ain't imported French champagne, folks," he told the crowd, as he filled a third mug. "Sech as Mr. Van Ruin guzzles ever' day down there in Washington City. Champagne, I might add, bought with hard-earned tax money, yers and mine. No sir! This here is plain o' Yankee hard cider—the very same that yer next presydent and vice presydent, Ginrel Harrison and Mr. Tyler, enjoy —an' it won't cost yuh a penny, nosiree. Compliments o' the Whig Party."

Culley caught the pale man's eye and called, "Hello, Lysander! How's that magazine of yours coming along?"

"Hello, Ford! Getting fatter every week, thank you!"

Lady Suffolk and her master went on by as the pale man grasped his suspenders with both hands, rocked back on his heels, and continued his address. "Now there's one thing I'm plaguey afeard of, folks. And that's a presydent who's too almighty proud ter use his own countrymen's products. Caterin' ter furriners. Sendin' our precious gold and silver out o' the republic by the boatload. . . ."

16

A (SLIGHT) TASTE OF GLORY

Culley drove Lady Suffolk onto the track. There, four drivers were "scoring" their horses—trotting them for short spurts around the course in a clockwise direction, to warm them up before the race. The liveryman drove over to the judges' stand to enter Lady Suffolk in the event.

"Three heats of one mile each," the presiding judge told him. "You reckon that little mare can go the distance?"

"And then some," Culley replied. "She has to get me back to Long Island tonight."

"You drove that horse over here from Long Island today?" one of the two other judges asked, full of skepticism.

"I did."

"And you're planning to race her this afternoon?"

"I am."

"And then drive her back to Long Island tonight?"

"Yes, sir."

"Yes, sir?"

"Yes, sir!"

"Yes, sir." The three judges exchanged a long, solemn, judicial look.

Two men were lounging against the rail nearby, gazing about them with a superior, slightly amused air, as though they knew perfectly well that they could buy and sell the whole course and everything and everybody in it, if they so desired—which they did not. Clearly, they were a pair of individuals who considered each other an equal but rated the rest of the world a notch or two lower. One of them, a short, stocky person whose square brown face was fringed by a stubby dark beard, strutted forward.

"I'm going to act a generous part, friend, and give you some advice," he told Culley. "Instead of racing that mare of yours, you ought to give her a rest. She's earned it."

"She hasn't earned anything, yet," replied the liveryman, irritated by the fellow's manner.

The second man swaggered over to join his companion. He was taller and much thinner, and his long, horsy face was decorated by a yellow handlebar mustache.

"Listen to what he tells you," he advised Culley. "He knows a little about horseflesh."

"A little," the first man agreed dryly. Turning back to the liveryman, he said, "The horse is an industrious animal, friend. He'll drive himself to death, if you let him."

"Not this horse," Culley replied. "She's all whalebone and wire."

"You're going to knock her off her legs, friend."

"Those legs are cast iron."

The two companions exchanged wry glances. They plainly were miffed that Culley did not show them the respect they so obviously felt was their due, but they chose to act amused. They returned to the rail, the stocky one remarking, "Every man must go to the devil by his own road."

"Do you know who you were talking to?" the presiding judge asked Culley in an awed voice.

"No," the liveryman replied carelessly. "Who?"

"He's generally known as 'The Napoleon of the Trotting Turf.' "

"Madison Wiles?"

"The very same."

Culley groaned. He asked, dreading the answer, "And the other?"

" 'The Old Field Marshal,' " the judge said, clearly enjoying the liveryman's discomfort.

"Leonard Toms?" Culley breathed, repressing a shudder.

"The very same."

That had been the answer the liveryman dreaded. For, if he had not known the two most famous whips of the turf by sight, he certainly knew who they were. Their names and nicknames, as well as the names of their horses, were household words in the nation.

"Ah well," he remarked with a feigned blitheness, "as Poor Richard tells us, 'There have been as great souls unknown to fame as any of the most famous.' "

"Meaning yourself," the judge said.

"The very same," Culley replied. Then a distressing thought popped into his head and he asked quickly, "Are they entered?"

The judge snorted. "Not them. They're just spectators today. They wouldn't bother themselves trying conclusions with *those* nags." He nodded toward the four horses trotting around the course. "Fifty dollars, please."

Culley stared at the judge in surprise. "Fifty dollars?"

"The entrance fee is fifty dollars a side," the judge explained patiently.

"Oh, of course," Culley said, paying up. Fifty dollars! He'd had no idea that harness racing was so expensive.

"*Those* nags," as the judge had called them, were four impressive animals, which Lady Suffolk and her master saw when they joined them in scoring. Jolly Roger, Princess Dot, Cannonball, and Tulip were all big horses, with bulging muscles and flaring nostrils. The numerous scars and welts from whips that covered their backs showed that all four were veteran campaigners. From the long, ugly spur scars on their flanks, they had also raced under saddle.

Culley didn't notice these souvenirs, however. What caught the liveryman's eye were the neat velvet jackets and the vivid silk caps of the other drivers, which made him feel like a bumpkin in his everyday clothes.

Jolly Roger's driver was all in black, the color of his stallion. As Lady Suffolk trotted up, he yelled to the driver of Princess Dot, a snow white mare, "This is going to look like a race between a filly and her mama and papa!"

The other reinsmen roared with laughter.

"Sir, a word of advice," the driver of the black called to Culley. "You'd best take a good look at my front now, because, when the race starts, all you'll see is my back!"

The other reinsmen laughed again, shouting, "That goes for me, too!" and "Yes, sir!"

"We'll make the honorable gentlemen sing out a little more on the other side of their mouths soon," the liveryman muttered.

When the drivers drew lots for post positions, however, Culley found himself "on the rim," the outside and the worst spot of all. Cannonball was the pole horse, next to the rail and in the best position. On the other side of him was Jolly Roger, then Tulip, and then Princess Dot.

"All right, gentlemen," the starter's bullmoose voice boomed through his megaphone, "turn your horses and score for the word. And don't you head that pole horse!"

The five men turned their trotters around, arranged in their post positions, and started them at a brisk pace toward the judges' stand. A line had been scratched across the dirt track there. His hand on a big iron bell, the starter was leaning out of the stand, straining to see if the five contestants were more or less abreast.

The four big horses were full of stall courage, fresh and eager to go. Lady Suffolk's exertions on the road to Brooklyn, followed by the forced inactivity aboard the ferry, had caused her muscles to stiffen. The scoring had loosened them, but it had also burned up energy she could not afford to give away at this time. Her pipes were open, however, her great heart was drumming, and the clamor and fever of the course called up that pluck of old.

Jolly Roger's driver was having difficulty holding the powerful black in. Just before the five horses crossed the scratch, the stallion lunged forward, breaking the symmetry.

A loud clang rang out.

"What's that?" Culley yelled to the driver of Princess Dot.

"The bell," the other man answered.

"What bell?" Culley asked. There was no reply. The

clang sounded again . . . and again. Culley had driven Lady Suffolk halfway around the track before it dawned on him that he and the little gray mare were the only ones racing. The other contestants had returned to the judges' stand. Turning her around, Culley drove Lady Suffolk back.

Twenty-six times, the starter summoned the horses. Twenty-six times, he had to sound the recall bell, as Jolly Roger or one of the other veterans shot ahead in the last few seconds. Each false start stole a bit more of Lady Suffolk's resources.

"All right, gents," the starter shouted, "turn for the word!"

Legs flashing, clipping off the distance in neat, square strokes, the five trotters approached the scratch abreast. The crowd, which had been holding its breath, sensed that the time had come and broke into an explosive roar, but the starter's sharp command sounded clearly above the din.

"Go!"

The five horses dashed forward, racing counterclockwise around the track, their drivers' whips sounding like a gun battle. The track was rough, fetlock-deep in dust and loose dirt, and was not graded on the turns, so that the sulkies skidded badly.

Cannonball took the lead and held it around the first turn, nearly to the quarter post. There, the pole threw a shadow across the track. Cannonball jumped over the shadow, breaking his stride. The other horses swept past him.

Lady Suffolk had lost all confidence in her driver. Culley seemed to have forgotten everything he had ever known about handling a trotter (which wasn't much to begin with). Delirious with excitement, he pulled on the reins, sometimes yanking them, and steadily plied the whip. Each lash took something out of the mare, but she continued to give the best that was in her.

Lady Suffolk saw Jolly Roger's driver edge the black over to the rail. One by one, the other two big horses to his right sidled inward, closing up the gap. The little gray mare was trotting well, very well indeed, but, on the outside, she had a greater distance to travel than any of the other horses, particularly Jolly Roger in his new position.

The flying dirt and dust got in her nose and stung her eyes. Half-blind and breathing with difficulty, she nonetheless held her own.

Approaching the half-mile post, Lady Suffolk saw something metallic fly off from Princess Dot, gleaming for a moment in the sunlight. The white mare had thrown a shoe. Rapidly, she fell behind. Culley brought the little gray mare into the other trotter's lane.

At the three-quarter post, it was Jolly Roger leading by a half a neck, followed by Tulip and Lady Suffolk. The mare was still trotting well, but she was tiring. Coming around to the head of the homestretch, Jolly Roger's sulky skidded wide, thrusting Tulip into Lady Suffolk.

Both horses broke. The mare recovered herself first, but, as she was going rough-gaited, a forefoot had shot up, slashing her belly. The drops of blood flew, splattering her driver and the sulky. That made the liveryman, in his frenzy, whip her all the harder.

Going into the home stretch, it was Jolly Roger by three lengths, followed by Lady Suffolk, with the other horses far behind.

[176]

The little gray mare took off after the big black stallion in a grueling, stern chase. The roar of the crowd was deafening. She sensed that the people weren't rooting for her, but, as she ate up the daylight between her and the black, the cheers changed to shouts of amazement and admiration.

Sixty yards from the wire, it was Jolly Roger by two lengths. Her head stretched out parallel to the ground, tail flowing behind, legs driving in a long, low, locomotive stroke, Lady Suffolk continued to come up on him.

At forty-five yards, it was Jolly Roger by a length and a half. The black's driver was hunched forward, as if cringing. Aware of the crowd's change in tone, he knew without looking back that the little gray mare was on his tail, and he whipped his horse steadily.

Thirty-five yards away, the three judges stood somberly in their stand, holding their watches. Thirty. Lady Suffolk passed the other sulky, then began to come up on the black.

He ran with his ears laid flat and his big eyes rolling. He rolled one back at the mare and they looked at each other— he wild-eyed and desperate, she calm and determined.

Twenty yards. Fifteen. Ten. It was Jolly Roger by a half a length, a neck, a head, a short head. The black stallion and the little gray mare crossed the scratch in a blanket finish.

At last Culley let up on the whip. Turning Lady Suffolk, he brought her back to the judges' stand, where the three officials were in solemn conference.

Then the presiding judge leaned down from the stand and called to Culley, "Sir, what was your mare's name again?"

"Lady Suffolk, sir!" The liveryman shouted it out for all

to hear, glancing about him to see the crowd's reaction.

The judge held his hand up for silence.

"Lady Suffolk and Jolly Roger—a dead heat!"

Culley groaned. He had been sure that he (not Lady Suffolk) had won. "Well, be it so," he remarked. "We still have two more heats."

There was a delay as Princess Dot's shoe was retrieved and nailed back on her hoof. Meanwhile, a steady stream of people came up to touch Lady Suffolk and exchange a few words with her master.

"I bet on the black the first time out," one man said, "but this time my money's riding on your mare."

"I've never seen such game and deep bottom, sir," another told Culley, shaking his hand.

"Thank you, sir," the liveryman replied, as modestly as he could manage, taking the remark as a personal compliment.

"Congratulations, friend. She's a splendid goer." It was Madison Wiles!

"You have a fine little mare there, sir," Leonard Toms said. "Take care of her."

"I will, sir, I will," Culley replied, his spirits soaring.

When the drivers drew lots for post positions in the second heat, Jolly Roger got the rail. Cannonball received the second lane, Princess Dot the third, and Lady Suffolk was fourth. Tulip was on the outside.

When the starter called them up, Lady Suffolk was still puffing. The other four horses were much fresher than she, but none was more eager. There was still plenty of trot in those gray legs, and she still had her pluck.

"Go!"

The five contestants took the word for a splendid start. Princess Dot immediately grabbed the lead and held it nearly to the half-mile post. But when she came to the point where she had thrown her shoe, she broke her stride, recovered herself, then did a double break. She was out of the race.

Jolly Roger surged to the fore, showing the others the back of his sulky. Cannonball was coming along fast. Lady Suffolk and Tulip were head and head behind them.

On the lower turn, the black stallion's sulky skidded wide, crashing into Cannonball's. Lady Suffolk saw something black spinning away—a wheel. At the same time, Cannonball's sulky fell on one side and his driver shot out from it, as if launched from a catapult. Landing on his face, the man lay still on the track, his head twisted to one side. He had bitten the dust.

The others rushed by. Terrified, Cannonball broke into a gallop, his wrecked sulky bouncing behind him.

Hoof by hoof, with her fine, bold, sweeping stroke, Lady Suffolk pulled ahead of Tulip. The strain reopened the slash on her belly, and the liveryman drove through a red rain.

Taking the lash at nearly each yard, her mouth tormented from the pulling and yanking on the reins, badly confused by her master's erratic behavior, rapidly nearing the point of exhaustion, the little gray mare dashed after the black stallion.

The crowd was hysterical. Lady Suffolk sensed that now the thunderous shouts were for her, and that helped a little. But the main factor that kept her going, and gaining on the black with every step, was her pluck, what the horse fanciers called her game and bottom.

The name sounded clearly now. "Lady Suffolk! Lady Suffolk! Come along, Lady Suffolk!"

Jolly Roger was three lengths ahead. Two. A length. The mare was coming up on his right. He rolled his right eye back at her, and she saw the fear there, and the burning hatred.

"Lady Suffolk! Lady Suffolk!"

On the turn going into the homestretch, the black stallion went too wide, his sulky swerving out almost to the middle of the track. The little gray mare slipped inside. She was now next to the rail, he on her right. The two raced neck and neck up the stretch, their drivers flogging them zealously.

"Lady Suffolk! Lady Suffolk!"

The people were jumping up and down, the men waving their hats, the women their handkerchiefs. The little gray mare was on the verge of collapse, but, hoof by leaden hoof, she moved ahead a half a length, a length, a length and a half. The finish was less than thirty yards away.

"Lady Suffolk! Lady Suffolk!"

Culley twisted in his seat to see the ladies, or to see if they were watching him. The sulky veered to the left, grazing the rail, and caused the mare to break her stride.

She recovered herself quickly, but Jolly Roger, in his square trot, passed her and won by a neck. She knew the race was over when Culley stopped whipping her.

The starter gave the call for the final heat. Lady Suffolk made it up to the mark, but was unable to go farther.

She stood with her head down between her knees, her entire body atremble, quivering in every muscle, dead beat.

[181]

She scarcely heard the soft exclamations of sympathy and shock that came in waves from the crowd.

Culley stepped down from the sulky and slowly led her through the murmuring crowd toward the Brooklyn ferry and home. But they had so long to go before they were home . . . so very long still to go before they were home.

17

A GREENHORN SEASON

Suddenly, summer was gone—just like *that*! Its casual, fancy-free breezes gave way to a low, rushing, insistent roar that rustled the green leaves and rattled the yellow and red ones that had already fallen to the ground. Fall was an apt name for the season. Where summer had seemed one long, slow day, now there were many, many days—each of them shorter than the one before—falling like the dead leaves as the land rushed headlong toward the end of the year.

Day by day, everything was moving faster, and there never seemed to be enough time for anything. To put the capper on the matter, that fall, "Brother Jonathan"—America—was embroiled in the wind-up of the most rip-roaring political carnival of the nation's history, the "log cabin and hard cider" campaign of 1840.

Day and night, the large, sensitive ears of Lady Suffolk were assaulted by the shriek of fifes, the rat-a-tat-tat and rub-a-dub-dub of drums and the ringing, never-ending battle cry:

Tippecanoe and Tyler, too!
Tippecanoe and Tyler, too!

At no time the one line, but always repeated:

Tippecanoe and Tyler, too!
Tippecanoe and Tyler, too!

Wherever her master drove her, there were pictures of General Harrison in the windows of shops and houses— woodcuts of him on a horse, behind a plow, in the doorway of a log cabin. Everywhere there seemed to be clambakes and barbecues, with barrels and barrels of hard cider.

At night, huge bonfires sprang up in the streets, sending towers of swirling orange sparks into the dark sky. There were torchlight parades, with miniature log cabins hauled in wagons and men on horseback carrying kegs at the ends of poles, the torches smoking and flaring in the autumn wind. And Lady Suffolk went to sleep each night hearing the Whig campaign song:

Farewell, dear Van,
You're not our man;
To guide the ship,
We'll try old Tip!

The little gray mare was submerged in the campaign, stormed by the hot wind of the orators. There were a few Democrats, dressed in formal black broadcloth and using correct English, but most of the speakers were Whigs, wearing the rustic get-up and drawling in the homespun terms of a stagecoach lawyer.

The race courses were political arenas. It was here that Lady Suffolk had to endure the most explosive bombast of the campaign.

The second heat of that race at the Beacon had changed the life of Ford Culley forever. Coming from behind and passing Jolly Roger, hearing the cheers of the spectators, and seeing their obvious admiration had given the livery-man something he had never had before. In so doing, it had afflicted him with an incurable case of Fetlock Fever. From that point on, the race course was Culley's primary interest in life.

The first thing he did on his return from the Beacon track was to hand Lady Suffolk over to Stephen Seven Trees and Jerry Bean, with instructions to put her in the best possible fix in the least possible time. The next thing he did was to have himself fitted for a gray velvet jacket and tight gray woolen trousers, the outfit to be topped off by a gray silk cap.

Then, with floor-pacing, finger-drumming impatience, he waited, day by day, for his costume to be ready and for Lady Suffolk to be put in the top of her form.

For the most part, Mary Culley watched her husband in stony silence. But one morning, when he brought the mare in from a series of rallies, she spoke up. "It really is a disease with you, isn't it?"

"It's not fatal, my dear," he replied.

"How do you know it isn't fatal?" she demanded. "You're not a young man, and you're not in the best of health."

"I'm in the prime of life and sound as a dollar."

"Speaking of dollars, where are we going to get the money to enter all these races?"

Her husband raised his finger, opening his mouth.

"And don't you dare give me one of those stupid Poor Richard sayings," she told him.

He lowered his finger, closing his mouth.

To Lady Suffolk, he remarked quietly, "I was just about to say, 'If your riches are yours, why don't you take them with you to t'other world?' "

As hardy as the little gray mare was, her day at the Beacon track—along with the going there and the coming back —had taken a great deal out of her, and Culley's outfit was ready well before she was. He wore it every day and, although he struggled manfully with the desire, it was nearly impossible for him to pass a mirror without giving his reflection a quick check.

Cracked and cloudy as it was, the glass in the stable registered his image more than any other because it was private. On occasion, however, Mrs. Culley invaded his domain, as did Meg all the time.

"Look at you! Look at you!" his wife exclaimed one day.

She had given him a start, but he pretended not.

"I am, my dear, I am," he replied easily.

"Primping and preening like a peacock in your little sulky suit."

In answer, he reached to the back of his head, pushing the cap forward, cocking it over one eye. His wife threw up her hands in exasperation and stalked out of the stable.

"My little sulky suit," Culley repeated dryly, getting a good side view of himself, pulling in his stomach.

"I think you look awfully nice, Papa," Meg told him.

He jumped, making Lady Suffolk snort nervously.

"Where'd *you* come from?" he asked. Calming down, he said, "Thank you, Trouble. I expect your mother thinks so, too. She just won't admit it. 'The proud,' you know, 'hate pride—in others.' "

"Poor Richard?"

"Poor Richard."

"You know something, Papa?" Meg asked. "You should take Stephen with you when you race Lady Suffolk."

"Why?"

"She does her best when he's with her."

"I'll think about it."

The Beacon hadn't changed much when Lady Suffolk returned there. The blackface musician was still hopping about on his little platform, frantically strumming his banjo. Dr. Cestus had gone elsewhere to read heads, but the orators were present in good voice.

"It's a death struggle, folks!" a stagecoach lawyer shouted. "A death struggle between log cabins an' palaces! Aye, between hard cider an' champagne!"

"Tippecanoe and Tyler, too!" the crowd chanted. "Tippecanoe and Tyler, too!"

Further on, a Democrat was addressing another group.

"Are the Whigs fighting for the right to live in log cabins?" he demanded. "Is there some tyrant in the republic who prohibits them from pulling down their mansions of granite and marble, and putting up log cabins in their place?"

Silence. Then the cry arose:

Tippecanoe and Tyler, too!
Tippecanoe and Tyler, too!

With Culley driving the little gray mare, and Stephen riding John Paul Jones, they made their way through the crowd to the track, where the liveryman registered Lady Suffolk in the race. Jolly Roger was not present, nor was Cannonball, but Tulip and Princess Dot were there, scoring, along with three other horses. All were highly rated.

To the surprise of everyone except Stephen and Culley —with the boy's care between heats counteracting her master's harsh treatment during them—Lady Suffolk took the race in three straight heats, winning the hundred-dollar purse.

"She's small, 'tis true, but she's considerable of a horse," one man commented.

"Considerable," another agreed. "I'd surely like to see what she could do against Pistol and Front Street."

In the weeks that followed, the talk of Lady Suffolk trying conclusions with the two top trotters in the nation grew steadily. Articles discussing such a contest began to appear in newspapers and magazines.

Meanwhile, Lady Suffolk was almost constantly on the road, traveling from one track to another. Her master drove her from the Beacon to the Hunting Park Course, in Philadelphia, back to the New Jersey track, up to the Cambridge Course, in Boston. . . . Except for Stephen's encouragement and careful handling, she would not have been able to stand the pace.

As it happened, however, she was winning races hoof over hoof, and her times kept getting better: two minutes and forty-three seconds for the mile; two minutes and forty-one; two-thirty-nine. Her fame spread, and the crowds came to see the little gray mare from Long Island.

"For a greenhorn horse and a greenhorn driver, we're not doing too bad," Culley remarked one chilly afternoon, following an unusually grueling race that Lady Suffolk had won with no help from him. "Not *too* bad."

"Yes, sir," Stephen replied, rubbing bear grease into the mare's whip cuts.

The boy's presence helped Lady Suffolk in another fashion. Except for him, Culley—that fierce competitor, that dunderhead—would have cheerfully raced her all the way to the tracks. But whenever they encountered another horse and driver going in their direction and the liveryman got that gleam in his eye, Stephen called out softly but firmly, "Mr. Culley!" And there was no brushing.

Voters in Maine went to the polls in September, and, soon afterward, the Whigs had a new campaign song. Wherever she went, Lady Suffolk was assailed with it.

> And have you heard the news from Maine,
> And what old Maine can do?
> She went hell-bent for Governor Kent,
> And Tippecanoe and Tyler, too,
> And Tippecanoe and Tyler, too!

For some time, the weather had been frosty and clear, with a layer of ice covering the water in the home trough each morning. Then, all at once, the air became as warm as in June, and a blue haze hung over the land.

"Indian summer," Meg remarked.

She was watching Stephen groom Lady Suffolk after her

morning workout. The little gray mare was in training for a race next week at the Centreville Course, on Long Island. Culley was particularly eager about this contest, since one of the entries was Jolly Roger.

Stephen put down the brush for a moment.

"The old people in our village said this weather came because a great *Manito*, the son of the West Wind, was visiting his kinsfolk on Long Island," the boy told her. "As he was passing by, he stopped to rest and built a fire that warmed the earth once more, and the smoke drifted down over the hills and fields and seashore."

"Oh, I like that!" Meg exclaimed.

He grinned. "I do, too."

The weather was still warm and hazy the day of the race. Culley and Stephen left early, so that Lady Suffolk would have time for a rest before the match. Mrs. Culley, Meg, and Jerry Bean saw them off. The liveryman was in high spirits.

"Mr. Culley!" Stephen warned.

Three times that morning, he managed to prevent the man from brushing before they arrived at the track. The Centreville Course was aptly named, for it was the center of harness racing on Long Island. All roads leading to the track were loaded with vehicles for miles. On both sides of the roads were streams of people, walking.

"There's Lady Suffolk!" the cry went up. "Huzza for the little gray mare!"

Trotting her smartly past, Culley took the cheers as if they were for himself. Stephen rode with eyes cast down in embarrassment. At the course, he watered Lady Suffolk and fed her a second breakfast of a quart of oats and a pound of hay. Then he groomed her, quietly singing his grooming song. As the time of the race approached that afternoon, she was well rested and eager to go.

There were six horses in the field. The drivers drew lots for post positions. The driver of a muscular little Irish horse named Loch Cohn drew the rail. Next to him was Yankee Dude, a rangy gray, then Bullhide, a stocky brown gelding. Lady Suffolk was in the fourth position, with Jolly Roger to her right.

On the outside was Cannonball, whose new driver was visibly nervous at being next to the horse and driver that had caused the death of his predecessor. To increase the man's agitation, Jolly Roger's driver kept glaring at him, muttering. The black stallion, himself, kept rolling his eyes, flashing looks of hatred at Lady Suffolk, who faced him calmly.

Looking on together as the drivers scored their trotters were Madison Wiles and Leonard Toms, both wearing their superior smiles, but not missing a thing. Each of the pair was entered in the second match that afternoon.

Seeing the two, a group of sports journalists moved in, pencil and paper ready. The questions were sharp and quick.

"Gentlemen, what is your opinion of Lady Suffolk?"

"She's one of the best, take her for all in all, of the trotters," Wiles promptly replied.

"Mr. Toms?"

"I agree with Mr. Wiles," the other driver said. "Properly handled, she'll show her heels to many a fast field."

"You don't think she's being properly handled?"

"Now I didn't say that."

"Is she, sir?"

"I have no reply to that question, sir."

"Would you gentlemen care to try conclusions with her?"

"I'll go to the post with her whenever her owner desires," Wiles answered.

"And I," Toms declared, adding with a chuckle, "He could enter her in the match with us this afternoon, if he cared to."

Like a pack of wolves, the reporters closed in on Lady Suffolk and her driver.

"Mr. Culley, Mr. Toms, and Mr. Wiles just suggested that you enter your mare against them in the second match this afternoon."

"Oh, they did, did they?"

"Are you going to ignore the challenge, sir?"

"Ford Culley never ignores a challenge, sir."

"Then you'll enter?"

"With all my heart, but I have another race first."

By the time the starter called the horses up for the first heat, the afternoon had turned muggy. At the word, Loch Cohn shot ahead and had a lead of three lengths at the half-mile, with the other horses bunched behind him. Then the Irish horse began to wilt in the strange humidity, and the others came up, passing him one by one.

On the lower turn, Yankee Dude led by a length, followed by Bullhide, Lady Suffolk, Jolly Roger, and Cannonball. The black stallion's sulky skidded wide on the turn, but Cannonball's driver was keeping a careful distance, even if it meant losing the race.

Going down the backstretch, Culley and Lady Suffolk made their move. Trotting with machine-like precision, the little gray mare moved up on Bullhide. On the turn going into the homestretch, she passed him.

Coming up the stretch, only Yankee Dude was ahead of her; but he was fading, and she was getting stronger with every stride, even though her wrought-up master was yanking on the reins and flogging her as fast and hard as his arm could move.

With three hundred yards to the wire, it was Lady Suffolk and Yankee Dude head and head. He stayed even with her for about a dozen strides, but then broke and fell back. She was alone in the hurricane roar of cheers. Culley stopped whipping her. Twisting in his seat, he shouted to the crowd, "What's the time?"

In twisting, Culley made the sulky swerve outward, breaking the rhythm of her stride. Jolly Roger came up fast on the inside. The little gray mare collected herself, and the two horses raced neck and neck toward the finish line, two hundred yards away.

Cleverly, so that the judges would detect no foul, Jolly Roger's driver began to crowd Culley, inching his sulky sideways until there was scarcely any space between the two—and still he came on.

"Take care!" Culley shouted.

Stephen, at the finish line, heard clearly over the cheering a series of sharp explosions. He saw the spokes of Culley's left wheel, broken by the other sulky's axle, shoot off like a flight of black arrows.

The rim of the wheel snapped and the sulky crashed on its left side, hurling Culley headlong through the air. After he hit the track, he did not move. Jolly Roger raced on to win. Yankee Dude, coming up from behind them, was able to leap over Culley, but the sulky crashed into the fallen man. It flipped over, spilling its driver.

Stephen had started to run when he saw the spokes flying. He couldn't seem to make his legs move fast enough, however, and Lady Suffolk, panic-stricken, dashed by him and down the track, with the broken sulky bouncing and banging behind her.

Men rushed out at her from both sides, trying in vain to grab the reins. Lady Suffolk's hurtling body knocked them every which way. Ears flat, eyes bugged, mad with fear of the rackety horror she was dragging, she raced almost completely around the track.

Nearing the site of the collision, she saw someone up ahead who looked vaguely familiar.

"Lady Suffolk, stop!"

She pricked up her ears. The name penetrated the clouds of panic, and she recognized it as her own. She knew that voice, too. And she knew the speaker.

It was the boy. He stood in the middle of the track with both hands upraised. She began to slow down. As wind scatters fog, the sight and sound of the boy dispelled her panic, and she came up to him quietly.

Unaware of the thousands of eyes turned on him, deaf to the exclamations of admiration, the boy unharnessed the sulky, then swung onto the mare's back and rode her to where some men had carried Ford Culley.

The liveryman sat with his back to the rail. He was ghostly white and breathing with much pain and difficulty.

His jacket was torn and the knees of his trousers were ripped.

Seeing Stephen, Culley said in a faint but nonetheless distinct voice, "I am a dying man. Farewell."

"Mr. Culley!" the boy exclaimed. Jumping off Lady Suffolk, he knelt beside the liveryman.

Culley gave him a wink, then murmured so that only Stephen could hear, "I'll be okay. I'm put in mind of Poor Richard's maxim, 'The things which hurt instruct,' and I've had my share of instruction today. Let's hope I've learned something."

18

ANOTHER OLD SCORE SETTLED

The following article appeared in a New York newspaper:

SAD AFFAIR AT CENTREVILLE

In the third heat of a match at the Centreville Course a few days since, as the field was coming up the home stretch, the sulkies of Jolly Roger and Lady Suffolk collided, and Mr. Culley was thrown to the ground.

Fears are entertained that the popular Lady Suffolk will never race again, since we understand that her owner will not let anyone else ride behind her. Mr. Culley received no broken bones from his fall and being run over by the sulky of Yankee Dude, but we have learned that later that day he suffered a heart seizure and is now at home in bed under a doctor's care. It is believed that his racing career is finished.

In recent weeks, the Gray Mare from Long Island has become the talk of the racing world. The annals of the turf furnish no parallel to the Lady's meteoric rise to fame. Never has a horse shown such thorough game and deep bottom. Never has a horse so captured the heart of the public.

If Lady Suffolk's trotting career is over, more's the pity, for the talk of late has been a match between her and Pistol and Front Street. It is the opinion of your humble scribbler that, if such an event ever came off, the Lady would far surpass all her previous heats and make "limping Time toil after her in vain." We believe that such a meeting would result in the breaking of the fabled two-and-a-half-minute mile.

Since the above was in type we have learned that Mr. Culley has entered Lady Suffolk in the second match at the Beacon this Saturday. He has, moreover, issued a challenge to Mr. Wiles, owner of Front Street, and Mr. Toms, owner of Pistol, for the following Saturday afternoon at the Centreville Course "rain or shine." From this we gather that Mr. Culley has fully recovered. He has our warmest congratulations and best wishes.

In spite of what the newspaper said, however, the livery-man was still suffering from the effects of his heart attack. The morning of the match at the Beacon, Stephen Seven Trees and Jerry Bean had to carry him downstairs and lift him into the sulky.

Meg Culley and her mother followed slowly behind. Their eyes were swollen and red.

"For the last time, Ford," Mrs. Culley said, "think of your daughter and me."

"Please, Papa," Meg pleaded. "Stay here, and let Stephen drive Lady Suffolk."

"My dear, I *am* thinking of you two," Culley told his wife. "With a few more races under my belt, we'll be rich."

"With a few more races under your belt, you'll be under the ground," Mrs. Culley replied. "Dr. Potter told you, if you didn't slow down, your life was at risk."

"Dr. Potter!" Culley snapped his fingers. "I don't care

that for Dr. Potter. A few hours abroad in this weather will do me more good than all his medicines and beef tea."

"Papa, did you hear what I said?" Meg asked. "Let Stephen drive her."

"No, Trouble," he replied. "Remember, 'If you'd have it done, go; if not, send.' "

"Poor Richard?" his daughter asked.

"Poor Richard."

"Oh, for mercy's sake!" Mary Culley exclaimed.

"Meg, these people are coming out to see *me*," Culley told her. "It would be a selfish act to disappoint them."

"They're coming out to see that little gray mare," his wife corrected him.

"And me," he replied. " 'Time is money.' I must be off. We can continue the discussion upon my return tonight. Come along, Stephen."

Reluctantly, the boy mounted John Paul Jones.

The balmy Indian summer morning did revive Culley, putting color back into his pale cheeks. By the time the Long Islanders arrived at the Beacon, however, it was afternoon and he was beginning to droop, although the cheers for Lady Suffolk picked him up for a while.

As he was registering the gray for the second event, a group of men came up to him. "We're backing your mare," one told him. "Pray, sir, stay on the ground today and let someone else ride behind her."

The others nodded agreement.

"Well, gentlemen, I certainly appreciate your concern," Culley replied, his chest swelling, "but I assure you, my health is sound as a dollar."

The men exchanged wry glances. This was not exactly

what they had in mind. One came out with it. "We have a good deal of money involved, sir."

"Your money is safe, sir," Culley replied. "Never forget, 'He that by the plow would thrive, himself must either hold or drive.' "

The glances were now downright glum, in sharp contrast to the happy shouts of the crowd of "There's Lady Suffolk!" and "That's the Little Gray Mare from Long Island!"

In the crowd, Lady Suffolk noticed a boy silently staring at her. She had seen that boy before.

Sensing the steady gaze, Stephen looked about and found the same boy. He knew that lad from somewhere, years ago. Thickset, with curly orange hair and small, mean-looking eyes, he was staring up at Stephen with an expression that was the far side of admiration.

With him was a man that Stephen guessed was his father, a wiry, bowlegged person with a round, bald head. His rolled-up sleeves revealed muscular arms. That man was familiar, too. The son began to whisper to another boy, whom Stephen had never seen before.

About the time that the orange-haired boy yanked on his foot, nearly pulling him out of the saddle, Stephen remembered who he was—Jimmy, the blacksmith's son.

Stephen sprang to the ground, facing his old adversary calmly, waiting for him to make the first move. Jimmy just glared at the Indian boy, anger screwing his eyes even smaller. Then Stephen felt a heavy blow in the side. The other boy had tackled him. The sudden thrust almost knocked Stephen down, but this boy did not carry as much weight as Jimmy, and Stephen was able to keep his feet.

[200]

Twisting to the side, he seized the other boy around the shoulders and, with a quick wrench, hurled him through the air. The boy landed off-balance on his heels, then sat down very hard on the ground, with a startled look and a loud grunt. Jimmy rushed forward.

"Give them room!" the blacksmith shouted to the crowd, quickly marking a circle in the dirt. "One down and the other come on—it's the Yankee way!"

Lady Suffolk saw Jimmy swing a roundhouse right. So did Stephen. With the technique Jerry Bean had spent so many long hours teaching him, he stepped inside the swinging fist, blocking it with his left, at the same time slamming a hard right into Jimmy's ribs.

"Ugh!" The grunt was audible above the yelling of the crowd.

Stephen gave the boy a left to the head and a right to the midsection before springing back. Lady Suffolk was snorting, stamping, neighing, her ears assailed by the shouts for the blacksmith's son.

"Go it, Red!" "Come along, Curlytop!" "Get that redskin!"

Jimmy charged, arms flailing. Stephen leaped to the side, smashing a left into the other boy's face as he blundered by, following it up with a right to the jaw. This was the one that did it. Jimmy's little eyes flew up toward the top of his head and his mouth hung loose. Momentum kept him going out of the ring. Then he stumbled and fell headlong in the dirt.

His friend was waiting at the edge of the ring, without quite the same enthusiasm he had shown earlier. He came in warily, hands out, circling. Stephen grabbed him and threw him with no trouble. He landed hard, the breath knocked out of him.

"Huzza for Stephen Seven Trees!"

It was a woman's voice, and familiar from the past. Following his ears, Stephen found his uncle's housekeeper, Mrs. Eller, in the crowd. She was smaller than he had remembered her, but she was still a good-sized woman. He waved, grinning, puzzled by her sudden look of dismay. Then he felt a stunning blow on the nose. Jimmy was back.

"Ah, he draws the claret!" the blacksmith shouted. "Go it, Jimmy! It's the Yankee way!"

Blood pouring from his nose, Stephen staggered backward. Jimmy charged in for the kill. Stephen leaped away. Jimmy charged again. Stephen jumped away once more. Jimmy took a deep breath, then rushed in a third time. Stephen started to spring back, then fell heavily to the ground. The blacksmith had tripped him.

"Hold!" Culley shouted. "That's not fair!"

Jumping out of the sulky, he rushed forward to help Stephen to his feet. The blacksmith grabbed him by the collar and yanked him back. Culley came on again, and the two men grappled as Stephen and Jimmy—a tangle of squirming arms and legs—rolled about on the ground. Stephen was holding his own, but Culley was no match for the blacksmith, who began, with keen enjoyment, to give him a thorough beating.

Then Lady Suffolk saw her old master, David Mercer, loom up. Whirling the blacksmith around with his left hand, the butcher presented his right. The one punch was all that was necessary.

It took Stephen three, but he accomplished the same end.

Father and son lay side by side on their backs, mouths open, eyes shut in a short, violent sleep.

"That redskin's considerable of a scrapper," someone in the crowd remarked.

"Considerable," another declared.

A third said thoughtfully, "I wonder how much white blood he has."

"I expect he don't have much of *any* kind left now," another replied with a chuckle.

Stephen stood by Lady Suffolk, arms around her neck. He felt that he was drawing strength from his "spirit guide." His nose has stopped bleeding at last, but it was swollen shut and he had to breathe through his mouth.

The butcher came over, shook hands with Stephen, and slapped the little gray mare on the shoulder. "I should have known I couldn't wear you out," he told her. "Toughest piece of horseflesh that ever looked through a bridle, I'll be bound. Whalebone and wire. Whalebone and wire!"

Culley walked up to the butcher. The rips in his velvet jacket, which his wife had so carefully mended, had come apart again, and his face showed evidence of the black- smith's fun, the bruises standing out all the more against the pallor.

"Poor Richard tells us that 'Most people return small favors, acknowledge middling ones, and repay great ones with ingratitude, sir," the liveryman remarked. "But I want you to know that I'll be in your debt the rest of my life."

The butcher hunched his shoulders. "A pleasure, sir," he replied—which was only the truth.

Turning to Stephen, Culley said, "I'm a bit weary. I believe I'll rest under yon oak until it's time for the race."

He walked unsteadily to the tree and lay down in its shade, covering his face with a handkerchief. Almost at once, the piece of silk began to puff up and fall back regularly. Stephen and Lady Suffolk stood by quietly as he slept.

Mrs. Eller came up and hugged Stephen. He did not seem to mind that very much. Then she patted Lady Suffolk, which the little gray mare didn't mind at all. The housekeeper and Stephen spoke in low tones, describing what had happened to each other since they had last been together.

Mrs. Eller had not ranged over as much territory as Stephen had, nor had her occupations been as varied as his. Her life, however, had been even more insecure than his, for, in 1840, the nation was still undergoing hard times.

In contrast to Stephen's various menial jobs in livery stables, on farms, and aboard steamboats, Mrs. Eller, for the most part, had continued as a housekeeper or cook on Long Island. Her first position after leaving Stephen's uncle had been with a former sea captain in Huntington. When his bank failed and he could not afford to keep her on, she cooked for the workers in a Brooklyn factory until it shut down. And so on.

"Now I'm working for a baker in Jamaica," she told the boy. "And, Stephen, we're going to get married!"

"You came down here all the way from Jamaica?" he asked.

"Yes, I read about the big race coming up and wanted to see if this was the Lady Suffolk I had known. I hadn't any idea that you would be with her. Stephen, aren't you glad?"

"That you came down here? I sure am."

"No, Stephen," Mrs. Eller said with a trace of her old asperity. "Glad that this baker in Jamaica and I are going to get married, as I mentioned."

"Yes." Which meant another hug.

A large, heavyset man and a boy came up then. The mare vaguely recognized both from the dim past.

"I said you'd be a champion some day, Lady Suffolk," the boy told her, patting her neck. To Stephen he remarked, "That wasn't a bad fight." Stephen grinned.

Then the mare remembered. It had been on a nippy fall morning, years ago, when she had been taken away from the life she had loved, the start of all her adventures. The big man was Joshua Desmond, the sheriff's deputy who had first owned her and who since had become sheriff. The boy was his son Josh. And the person who had taken her from that happy life was the man who called himself Bill Billings.

That warm Indian summer afternoon at the Beacon, the sheriff discussed Stephen's uncle with the boy and Mrs. Eller, at length. Explaining that he had recently returned a fugitive from justice to Nashville, Tennessee, Joshua Desmond showed them a piece of a handbill he had picked up there:

REWARD
$500

Will be paid by the Governor of Tennessee for the apprehension of WILLIAM HARNETT, wanted for stagecoach robbery and escape from prison.

HARNETT is about six foot three inches high—of a very thin make—and is about 40 years old. He has black hair and sunken blue eyes. His back is badly scarred up, and his left thumb is branded with the letters "HT." When he went away from the State Penitentiary he had on a striped nankeen coat. . . .

The rest of the handbill was torn off.

"That surely sounds like Mr. Billings," his former housekeeper remarked. "It surely does."

"Sir, what does 'HT' mean?" Stephen asked.

Josh Desmond answered for his father. "Horse thief."

"Horse thief!" Mrs. Eller exclaimed. "That explains the white gloves!" she remarked to Stephen, adding softly to herself, "I knew he was lying—*Hoover Tavern* indeed!"

"I looked up Harnett's alias Billings's record in the Nashville courthouse," Sheriff Desmond told them. "He stole a horse from Lynch's Stand, a wilderness inn on the Natchez Trace—claimed it was his own horse that Lynch had taken from him while he was asleep by the side of the trail, and he might have been telling the truth, as Lynch's reputation was not of the best.

"In all events, Harnett, alias Billings, was sentenced to receive thirty-nine lashes on his bare back, to be branded with 'HT,' to be exposed in the pillory for three days, and to serve twelve months in prison."

"Thirty-nine lashes!" Stephen exclaimed, thinking of Lady Suffolk's back after a race—and she had a thick pelt to protect her.

"When he came out of prison, he was a hardened criminal," Sheriff Desmond told them. He did some coining—counterfeiting—and there's a suspicion out that he was a member of John A. Murrell's Mystic Clan. He took to robbing stagecoaches. One he tried to hold up ran him down and broke his leg."

Mrs. Eller glanced at Stephen. "That's why he hated stages so! I *thought* he was a little exalted in the head on that subject!"

"He was captured and sentenced to ten years in prison," the sheriff went on. "But he nearly killed a guard and escaped. He has been at large since. Have either of you seen him recently?"

Gazing at each other solemnly, Mrs. Eller and Stephen shook their heads.

"Keep alert," Sheriff Desmond advised. "You just might."

The first event was in five heats. There was a great deal of scoring and there were many false starts, so that, by the time the second match was called, the red sun was low in the west, sending long violet shadows across the motionless grass of the Newark Meadows. It had become unpleasantly warm, not a breath of air stirring.

Ford Culley had slept the entire time. He arose at once when Stephen called him. Lady Suffolk watched as he came over to the sulky. His step was firm, but his face was white. Looking back, she saw him put his foot on the iron bar and pull himself up by the wheel.

He stood, balanced with one foot on the bar for a long moment, then gasped, clutching his chest, and went straight back like a falling tree.

Stephen ran forward and caught him before he hit the ground. Culley lay still, breathing with difficulty, an embarrassed smile on his moist, pallid face, for a crowd had gathered around them.

"Keep back!" someone yelled. "Give him air!"

When Culley spoke, he sounded like a frog. " 'Experience keeps a dear school, yet fools will learn in no other.' "

"What did he say?" an onlooker asked.

"Hold your tongue!" another snapped.

"Take the whip, Stephen," Culley croaked. "You ride behind Lady Suffolk today."

"Please, sir," the boy replied. "I expect I'd best stay with you."

"Do as you're told, Stephen, I'll be okay."

"Let me through!" The command came from a man who sounded as though he was used to being obeyed. "I'm a doctor!"

The crowd parted and a man in a top hat with a black bag came through. Kneeling by Culley, he picked up the liveryman's wrist and checked his pulse.

"Go ahead, Stephen," Culley ordered. "Wait, you forgot the whip!"

"No, sir, I didn't forget it," the boy replied.

There were four other horses in the match: Jolly Roger, eyes rolling just as crazily as ever; a brown mare from Vermont named Mountain Maid; a gray Scottish gelding named Thistle; and Blind Barney, a long black bag of bones with blurry white eyes and hoofs the size of tree stumps.

The sun set in great banks of purple and red clouds, but the temperature did not drop and all was perfectly still. A thunderstorm was approaching, and thick black rain clouds came rolling toward them over the Hudson River.

The first heat was run in almost total darkness. Mountain Maid on the inside led to the quarter pole, but then the others came up on her. At the half-mile, it was Thistle by a length, closely pressed by Lady Suffolk and Jolly Roger, with Blind Barney and Mountain Maid far in the rear.

In the homestretch, it was Lady Suffolk and Jolly Roger, head and head, neck and neck, to the sound of the whip cracking, as the black's driver lashed him steadily. The vast experience of Jolly Roger and his driver counted for much, but the little gray mare was trotting as she had never trotted before—able to put all her energy into the race and not have to endure the whip. She had complete confidence in the boy, just as he had in her. It was similiar to those nights so long ago when he used to ride her, and they were like a single unit.

Fifty yards from the wire, Jolly Roger broke and the little gray mare won going away. Time: two minutes and thirty-three and a half seconds.

Stephen went to check on Ford Culley. The liveryman sat propped up by the oak under which he had slept that afternoon. The doctor had given him a drink of brandy that eased the pain in his chest and boosted his morale. The little gray mare's victory helped, too.

In the second heat, Lady Suffolk was boxed in by the other horses for most of the race, and Stephen did not know what to do about it. Blind Barney won, with the little gray mare second. Time: two minutes and thirty-five seconds.

By the time the third heat was called, the track was in complete darkness and the judges had to light candles to see their watches.

Lady Suffolk, on the inside, led the field by a length at

the quarter pole. At the half-mile pole, she had increased her lead to a length and a half, fighting off Mountain Maid, Thistle, and Jolly Roger in quick succession, as they all dashed through the black night.

Overhead, there was a brilliant zigzag blaze of forked lightning, followed almost immediately by an explosion of thunder. In the blue flash, the entire countryside was vividly revealed. Startled, the little gray mare broke her stride, and Jolly Roger and Thistle swept past her. Recovering almost at once, she overtook them and again led the field.

The wind blew a hurricane. Rain fell in torrents. The five trotters rushed into a howling, drumming darkness, shot through with flashes of lightning, which showed that the track was now more a canal than anything else.

Lady Suffolk began to slip and slide with every step. Blind Barney, the rain splashing in his sightless eyes, came up on her and, as much at ease as a duck in a pond, passed her, going on to win by two lengths.

As the drivers were sitting in their sulkies in the rain, waiting for the time to be announced, Jolly Roger edged over to Lady Suffolk. Then, rocking back on his hindfeet, he let fly with his forefeet, kicking the mare in the right forearm, just above the knee.

Stephen pulled her away, hardly aware of what had happened, deaf to the announcement from the judges. For, in a blaze of lightning as they were coming down to the wire, he had seen someone in the crowd. He couldn't be sure whether it was his imagination or not, but it seemed to him that he had seen his Uncle Bill.

19

BEDLAM

Like a puff of smoke, the Indian summer vanished in the thunderstorm, and iron winter clamped down upon Long Island. Early the morning after the storm, Stephen began to train Lady Suffolk for her race with Front Street and Pistol, the following Saturday.

He took her on a series of short brushes and, for him, merry rallies. Her great heart was throbbing and, like a pair of leather bellows, her mighty lungs sent the vapor jetting in clouds from her nostrils. She should have been in high spirits. However . . .

"She's not herself, Jerry Bean," Stephen told the old Negro as they were unhitching the little gray mare after one of these sessions.

"Reckon she took cold last night?"

They blanketed her up and started to walk her.

"Getting wet has never bothered her before," Stephen replied, puzzled.

"Most people believe that a horse, if there's nothing ailing him, is as good one day as another," Jerry Bean told the boy. "But this just ain't so, 'specially with a race. To win, there's always a mixture of favorable conditions—weather, track, driver, and the ability of the opponents."

"Yes," Stephen murmured, thinking about his opponents Saturday. Front Street and Pistol, driven by the two best whips in the nation, shared the record for the mile: two minutes and thirty-one and a half seconds.

"And, of course, the horse must be right in tune, keyed up to the highest pitch," Jerry Bean went on. "But it's plain nonsense to expect all these matters to combine nicely every time a horse trots. And yet a great many people do expect this, and, after a race is lost, fall to cursing the horse and his driver."

"I'm worried, Jerry Bean," Stephen told him. "We've got five heats Saturday."

"What are you worried about?" Meg Culley asked, coming up to them. She was bareheaded, and the wind swirled her long hair about like a yellow flag. "Stephen, what are you worried about?"

"Lady Suffolk," the boy replied. "She's not acting right."

"How's she acting?" Meg asked.

"I don't know, but I can feel it. She's not herself."

"I wouldn't worry, Stephen," Jerry Bean told him. "We know she's all horse, and you've already put the right distance into her. I believe it's better to go easy now than to knock her off her legs with too much work."

"Five days to the meet," the boy remarked.

The next day was Tuesday. Since Culley had sent Jerry Bean on an overnight trip to Jamaica for supplies, Stephen was alone in the stable, so he arose even earlier than usual, to be able to handle all the chores.

First, he sent the hay and oats racing down the chutes from the loft to the mangers of the individual horses. Dust and bits of hay flew about like clouds of tiny insects, golden in the early light, before being caught by the cobwebs that hung like ragged gray curtains from the rafters and stanchions.

When Stephen came to clean Lady Suffolk's stall, he saw that she had barely touched her breakfast. Just before the noon feeding, Culley came to inspect the stable and to discuss the condition of the horses.

"Lady Suffolk's off her feed," the boy told him.

Culley shrugged. "Some of the best races are run by horses that are just beginning to get dainty, picking at their oats," he replied.

"Mr. Culley, I believe she's out of fix."

"She's fine drawn and wiry, Stephen. I reckon you've been too easy with her. You can't mollycoddle a horse. The horse, Stephen, is a humbug. You can ruin him with too much kindness."

"That's what my uncle said," Stephen replied.

"A little whalebone and whipcord properly applied can be very beneficial," Culley went on.

"That's what my uncle said."

"For dinner, give her two parts oats to one part bran, with a few carrots cut up in it," the liveryman told him. "Then hitch her to the sulky. I'm going to give her some brushing this afternoon."

The little gray mare ate more of her dinner than she had

her breakfast, but she did poorly in the brushes, even though her owner kept encouraging her with the whip.

Late that night, Stephen was awakened by the nervous snorting and stamping of the horses below. A Long Island winter wind blustered and boomed around the eaves, but the boy sensed that something else was disturbing the animals. Lighting the stable lantern, he climbed down the ladder, to see what was causing the hubbub.

The swinging lantern made the shadows jump back and forth. This movement bothered the horses even more. The most nervous of them all by far was the little gray mare. Stephen went over to her stall, spoke to her softly, entered, and stroked her soothingly.

The boy did not see the tall, dark form loom up, but Lady Suffolk did and gave a fearful snort. Stephen turned— in time to see the scarecrow figure of his Uncle Bill and the white-gloved right hand at the end of a long black arm swinging toward him.

The boy ducked, and the fist thudded into the oak wall of the stall. With a cry of rage and pain, the dealer struck out with his left, the one with the "HT" brand. Stephen sprang back, deeper into the stall, feeling the wind of the swinging fist that came short of his jaw only by inches. He crashed into Lady Suffolk's manger and fell, stunned momentarily, to the straw, dropping the lantern.

Billings tossed a noose around Lady Suffolk's head and began to pull her out of her stall.

"You can keep your land, Dog," he snarled. "This mare will do Bill Billings fine!"

Lady Suffolk saw the boy push himself up so that he was

on his hands and knees, facing her and her old master. She saw something else and screamed with terror.

The lantern had overturned in the scuffle, and the flaming whale oil was spreading out over the straw, setting it afire. Billings yanked on the rope. Stephen sprang forward. His uncle knocked him down. Shaking his head to clear it, the boy picked himself up and again sprang forward.

At that moment, Lady Suffolk rolled onto her forefeet and lashed out with her hindfeet, catching the dealer in the chest, hurtling him across the aisle and crashing into a stanchion. Like a sack of oats, without so much as a grunt, he plopped to the floor and lay still.

The few seconds that had passed were enough to drastically change the situation in the stable. Most of the straw of Lady Suffolk's stall was ablaze now. Fiery bits were flying around in the wind. Flames were licking up one side of the stall to the manger and curling around it as if it were a log in a fireplace.

The stable walls and floor were brick, but the stalls, stanchions, rafters, and ceiling were wood—wood that was old and dry. Also, each stall had a thick layer of straw and the wind carried a thousand tiny torches from the bonfire in Lady Suffolk's stall throughout the building. Almost at once, fires sprang up in a half-dozen different stalls.

Flames ate their way up the dusty, hay-stuck cobwebs and soon were at work in the loft. The stable was a bedlam of thick, creamy, blinding, choking smoke, swirling with painful sparks, and loud with the stamping, kicking, snorts, and screams of terrified horses.

Lady Suffolk seemed more frightened than any of the others. With all his might, Stephen tried to drag her down the aisle to the doorway and safety, but her brain was befogged and she balked.

Sparks landed on them, burning like brands. Every second, the smoke grew thicker, the flames hotter. Stephen knew that, in minutes, the stable would be a furnace. He could not budge the mare. There was one possible way to save her. Just one . . .

He ran, stumbling, to the door, unbarred it and swung it open. The cold, fresh air hit him like a blow in the face, and he breathed deeply, clearing his lungs. He ran back to Lady Suffolk. She was in the same spot where he had left her, stamping and screaming.

He leaped upon her back, sitting just behind her withers, perfectly balanced. She felt the familiar gentle but firm pressure of his knees and heels on her barrel, and she began to calm down.

No command was necessary. She trotted forward smartly, paying little attention to the fiery, smoky tumult around her. And then they were out of it and in the cold, dark night. Stephen tethered her to a rail a safe distance away and returned to the stable.

By this time, the fire was roaring through the hay-filled loft. Stephen started up the ladder, then jumped back to the floor. There were seven other horses in the stable. He began to take them out, one by one. First, John Paul Jones.

The flames had singed the horse in several places, adding to his terror. He was tossing his head, but Stephen was finally able to get a noose around his neck. He coaxed the animal, tugging gently on the rope. But, mad with fear, John Paul Jones fought him, and Stephen had to leap back to avoid his flashing hoofs.

He could see the flames reflected in the horse's bulging eyes, and he thought of Blind Barney. The lightning the other night hadn't bothered him a bit—because he couldn't see it.

Stephen got a blanket and threw it over John Paul Jones's head. The horse quieted down enough for the boy to lead him outside. Stephen tethered him to the rail next to Lady Suffolk.

The blanket was smoldering. Stephen dunked it in the trough, then jumped in himself. He gasped. The water was numbingly cold, but gave some protection against the oven heat of the stable. He pushed back inside, the dripping, steaming blanket wrapped around him, and went to Frigate's stall.

In some parts of the ceiling, blue flames jetted down between the boards, and there was a driving rain of sparks. Most of the rafters were ablaze; some of the stanchions were already smoking. A piece of burning board fell, striking the boy on the shoulder. It looked like some of the rafters would start to fall soon.

By covering their heads with the blanket, Stephen was able to get Frigate and the five other horses out. Again, he dunked himself and the blanket and, with it wrapped around him, returned to the stable.

Most of the stanchions were ablaze now, and the ceiling was falling in sections.

The ladder was smoking and blistered his hands as he climbed to the loft. There was enough light from the flames, but the smoke was so thick that he could see only a crimson glow.

Coughing, choking with every breath, he crawled on his

hands and knees across the hot floor to his cot. Reaching underneath, he grabbed the wolf pelt. It was smoldering but intact.

He climbed down several rungs of the ladder, then jumped. The smoke and heat were suffocating. He tripped over something—a body. Uncle Bill! In the uproar and stress of rescuing the horses, Stephen had completely forgotten him.

A rafter fell with a crash and an eruption of sparks. Any moment now, the entire roof would come down. Stephen felt his uncle's heart.

The beat was slow, very slow—and weak. Though alive, Billings was still unconscious and had not moved from where Lady Suffolk's kick had tossed him.

Stephen rolled his uncle onto the blanket. Placing the wolf pelt on the man's chest, he grasped the blanket with both hands and began to drag it, crouched over, walking backward.

Pieces of burning wood fell around them and on them. The heat was almost unbearable, and to breathe was next to impossible. Stephen's throat and lungs felt as though he were inhaling fire directly.

The blanket began to smoke. So did the clothes of Stephen and his uncle. A rafter crashed. Stephen was staggered by a falling board. He glanced over his shoulder but could see nothing in the smoke. He could not keep going much farther . . . much longer. He was on the point of collapse. Another rafter crashed. He could make three or four more steps, and that would be all.

"Stephen!"

It was Meg's voice. She sounded quite close.

"Are you all right?"

Next thing he knew, she had hit him with a bucket of frigid water. It felt delightful. It also put out the flames spreading across his shirt.

Meg was with her mother and father. They were wearing coats over their nightclothes. Meg held another coat in her arms. With a thunderous roar and a great swirling tower of sparks, the stable roof fell in.

After the blistering heat, between the bucket of water and the winter wind, Stephen was badly chilled. Meg handed him the extra coat, saying, "It's one of Papa's. I brought it for you."

Some of the water had struck Billings. He stirred, blinking up at Stephen in the flickering light. Then, with a snarl, he leaped to his feet, cocking his fist.

"Hold!" Culley shouted, rushing forward.

Billings thrust him aside, then turned back to his nephew. There was no spring left in Stephen's legs. He had no strength even to duck. He waited for the blow.

"Stand still or die!"

Sheriff Desmond came running up, followed by his son. The sheriff was holding a long-barreled revolver, which he clapped to Billings's head.

"We had a hunch he was somewhere around here," young Josh told Stephen. "We came as soon as we saw the fire. What! Why are you all wet?"

As briefly as possible, Stephen told him what had happened. Then Josh and his father marched off their prisoner. In the light of the flickering flames, Meg pointed to the wolf pelt bundle.

"After all the hubbub about that wampum, Stephen,"

she remarked, "I expect you'd better let my father keep it for you until you're ready to take over the Bee's Nest."

"I'll put it in my strongbox tonight," Culley told him.

Stephen thanked him, then went to Lady Suffolk.

20

THE WORD

Wednesday, the day after the fire and three days before the race, Lady Suffolk began to limp. She was staying, with John Paul Jones and Frigate, at a farm about a mile down the road from the Culleys' place. The other horses were being boarded in town.

"Lady Suffolk's gimpy in the right leg," Stephen Seven Trees reported to Culley Wednesday morning.

"Where in the right leg?"

"Here in the forearm, above the knee."

"How'd it happen, do you reckon?"

"I expect it's the kick she got from Jolly Roger last Saturday."

"And it's just showing up now?"

"Probably she has an infection that's been getting worse every day," the boy replied.

"Well, use the liniment and any Montauk Mumbo Jumbo you might have," Culley told him. "Time is money, and we have only three days. Lady Suffolk *must* race Saturday. After that fire, I can't afford to pay forfeit."

"Yes, sir."

"That's five thousand dollars, Stephen."

"Yes, sir."

"Stephen," Meg said later, as he was grooming the mare, "if she has an infection, can't you open it and let it drain?"

The boy finished combing Lady Suffolk's long, flowing tail. "No."

"Why not?"

"I believe the real infection is not where this little lump is but deep in her forearm, behind a tendon."

"Well, can't you go in there with a knife?"

"Feel her here," he said.

Meg laid her hand gently on the mare's forearm. She felt the slow, insistent beat as Lady Suffolk's great heart pumped the blood through her body. The mare snorted nervously.

"The horse's forearm is a big tangle of tendons and nerves and blood vessels," Stephen told her. "If I went in there with a knife, I could cripple her, or even make her bleed to death."

"Hmm. . . . Stephen, why did your uncle want to steal Lady Suffolk? What could he do with her? A horse as famous as she is, people would recognize her right away."

"Yes, she's famous now, but she wasn't a short time ago."

"You reckon that's why he didn't try to steal her before?"

"I think my uncle forgot all about Lady Suffolk after he sold her to that butcher, and it wasn't until she started to win races and there were stories about her in the newspapers that he thought about her again. Perhaps he thought that the race mare was another horse with the same name. I expect last Saturday was the first time he saw her in a race, and when he saw me behind her, he knew she was the same horse."

He was out of breath. Meg chuckled. "That's about the longest speech you've ever made," she told him. "But, Stephen, what could your uncle do with such a famous horse?"

"Give her a new name and race her in the West, where she would not be as well known."

"But people would recognize her."

"Not if he cropped her mane and tail and dyed her some other color."

"Ah!" She was silent for almost a minute, an unusually long time for her, as Stephen rubbed liniment on the mare's legs. Then Meg asked, "Well, what are you going to do to put Lady Suffolk back into good fix?"

"Keep grooming her and using liniment."

"That's all?"

"Yes. I believe it's mainly up to her." Straightening, he patted the mare on the neck, and she pressed her head down on his shoulder with a snort.

The abscess behind the tendon over Lady Suffolk's right knee was not large but it was hard and deep, like an inner boil. To put any weight on that leg was extremely painful, and she did it only for the boy.

By Friday, it was obvious that the little gray mare could not race in her condition, but Stephen and Jerry Bean continued to talk about the upcoming match as if she were going to race, as if they could hold off doom by brave words.

"The driving begins before the horses are called up to the mark," the old Negro said. "Before a race, the good driver knows not only all about his horse but also the strengths and weaknesses of the other horses."

"I didn't think Pistol and Front Street had any weaknesses," Stephen replied, rubbing warm liniment on Lady Suffolk's legs.

"Oh, yes, oh, yes," Jerry Bean answered. "Pistol, for example, is fast—faster than Lady Suffolk for a short distance, I'd guess—but she can take the starch out of him by pressing him hard. The speed of a speedy horse drops quick when he begins to tire."

Pistol was actually a nickname, the Negro told Stephen. The coal-black horse with the narrow white stripe down his face was really named Spanish Gold. His father was the famous Spanish stallion, Morocco. He earned the nickname because, at the word "go," he was off like a pistol shot.

"What about Front Street?" Stephen asked.

"She's a pacer, and pacers are generally figured to be a second or so faster than a trotter in the mile. They call her 'The Yardstick,' because of her exact way of going. Most of her races she wins by coming up from behind. She has a terrific finish."

"What can we do about that?" Stephen wanted to know.

"That's the way to think!" Jerry Bean exclaimed, with a broad smile. "It's not 'I' and 'she,' but 'we'—you and Lady Suffolk together. When y'all come up to the mark, y'all are one."

"But what can we do about Front Street and her finish?" the boy continued to question his knowing friend.

"Get ahead of her at the start and just stay there, that's

all. I reckon you'll get the most trouble from Pistol in the early heats and from Front Street in the later ones."

"What about the other entries?"

"Well, you know about Jolly Roger and his driver. It's considerable seldom that a reinsman like that is allowed to keep on racing after all the foul driving he has done. And beware the horse that rolls his eyes like Jolly Roger does. Any chance he gets, he'll kick or bite. Just steer clear of that pair."

"Isn't there another entry?"

"Hussar," Jerry Bean replied. "I don't know much about him. I know he's a puller. His driver leans back in the seat and takes a turn of the reins around his hands. People talk about a steady bracing pull, but many times I've seen horses tire under it without trotting their best. My advice to you with Hussar is to press him hard so he burns his powder fighting with his driver."

"What about us?" Stephen asked.

"You and Lady Suffolk? Y'all have been a tall time coming along together. I reckon y'all know each other just about as well as any horse and driver going."

Crouched by her right foreleg, Stephen gazed up at the little gray mare. Turning her head, she gazed down at him.

"I reckon there are a few pointers I could give you, though," Jerry Bean went on. "First, in a tight squeeze, with a generous horse like this one, the bit is the thing to win with. You talk to her through the leather telegraph. To keep her mouth alive, shift the bit every once in a while. Just a half turn of the wrist, like this, is enough to keep her alert."

"Like this?" Stephen asked, turning his wrist.

"Like that. She's inclined to break when she's tired. Watch her ears. A twitch of the ears signals a coming break. When you see that, just shift the bit, like this, and it will make her alert again and she won't break. Just shift the bit, like this."

"Like this."

"In the home stretch, even though she seems to be at the top of her speed, just shift the bit, and she'll let out another link. Just shift the bit, like this."

"Like this."

"Another thing. If the other horses have you boxed in, like they did at the Beacon last Saturday, pull Lady Suffolk back, then go to the outside. Most horses in such a situation would lose their will to win or, at least, break their stride, but I believe this little mare has too much game and bottom."

"Thank you, Jerry Bean," Stephen said. "I'll remember that."

"There's an old racing expression, 'Wait and win.' Some drivers like to take second or third place on the rail, putting the lead horse in the 'wind break' position. But there's much to be said for a fast start, since the lead horse can take the part of the course his driver wants, no matter what post position he drew."

"I understand you."

"You don't want to stay on the outside for the whole race ever," Jerry Bean told the boy. "A horse thirty feet out from the rail must travel more than a hundred yards farther to do his mile than a horse on the rail."

"That's good to know," Stephen replied thoughtfully.

"I've paced it off myself. One final point. If there is one

thing a driver must do, it is to turn a stone deaf ear to the bragging of his opponents. Don't let the other drivers scare you or make you mad, for Lady Suffolk will sense this and react to it."

"I'll remember," Stephen promised.

He had finished rubbing the little gray mare's legs with liniment. Straightening, he stood in front of her and said softly but urgently, "Come along, Lady Suffolk!"

Eyes on the boy, she trotted forward—or tried to. The pain in her right foreleg was severe—so intense that she stumbled and almost fell. It was impossible for her to do anything but walk on that leg, and even walking was painful in the extreme.

Stephen and Jerry Bean exchanged worried glances. Then the boy and the horse gazed at each other.

Saturday morning broke frosty and clear, without a ghost of a cloud. Lady Suffolk was, if anything, worse. Ford Culley studied her glumly.

"We'll take her in the wagon," he said. "We've got to make an appearance, and there's always the chance that something will come to pass. But let us remember, 'Diligence is the mother of good luck.' "

Mary Culley raised her eyebrows at this, but said nothing. She, Meg, and Culley were in their Sunday best. Mrs. Culley and her daughter each wore a gray ribbon on her coat. They climbed into the buggy. Stephen and Jerry Bean put Lady Suffolk into the wagon and they all set off.

The procession was a sad one. First came the buggy, then the wagon, with Jerry Bean driving Frigate and an old plodder that Culley had borrowed from the farmer who was boarding his horses. The sulky bounced along be-hind them. Stephen Seven Trees brought up the rear, rid-ing John Paul Jones. He was ill at ease in the gray velvet uniform and cap that Mary Culley had made for him.

Miles before they came to the Centreville Course, they encountered a triple line of omnibuses, carriages, buggies, coaches, wagons, cabs, and carts, all headed for the track. A large number of the women and girls wore gray ribbons.

"There's Lady Suffolk!" someone shouted, and all eyes turned toward the mare.

"She can't be Lady Suffolk," someone else remarked. "That horse is riding, and Culley always *drives* Lady Suffolk to the races."

By the time the Culley party arrived at Centreville, it was already overflowing with people, horses, and vehicles. The stands were crammed. Carriages, with their haughty Negro and white drivers sitting like stone statues, extended entirely around the inside of the track, lined up along the rail. The balcony of the clubhouse was packed. It seemed impossible for anyone or anything else to fit into the course, and yet they kept coming . . . and coming.

When Stephen and Jerry Bean brought Lady Suffolk down from the wagon and hitched her to the sulky, she was walking on three legs. Culley went off and returned with the proprietor of the course, a small, elderly man with a long white beard and a woebegone face.

"More's the pity," he remarked. "The betting has been a horse to a hen on Lady Suffolk. Of course you realize that she'll have to pay forfeit, not being up to the mark."

From his wretched expression, it seemed as though the $5,000 was coming out of *his* pocket.

"Of course."

"More's the pity," the proprietor repeated. "We have a good fast track for you today—hard and dry, the kind she likes best. I really had expected history to be made here this afternoon."

"Yes."

"More's the pity. You can see she's fine drawn and wiry but in no wise stale. Her eye is bright, her coat sleek, and her spirit eager."

"More's the pity," Culley agreed.

In the judges' stand, the starter raised his megaphone and shouted, "Calling all horses for the two-thirty trot!"

"The people will be greatly disappointed if the Lady doesn't race," the proprietor said. "I wonder if you would mind having your driver take her past the stand, so they can see her bad fix."

As the little gray mare hobbled past, the gasps and groans and sighs began in a soft murmur and swelled to a roar. The sympathy of the crowd, however, did not extend to some of the drivers.

"So that's the famous Lady Suffolk," the driver of Hussar shouted as he passed by, scoring his stallion. "She'd just make a breakfast for my horse!"

Silently, Stephen looked over at Hussar. He was a big, bulky roan that wore a pad on his belly band. The boy noticed that the stallion had a bold stroke, bending his knees sharply so that he nearly struck the pad every time he threw a forefoot up under him.

He also noticed that, as Jerry Bean had said, Hussar's driver leaned far back in his seat, a turn of the reins twisted around his hands.

"Too bad, Tecumseh!" Jolly Roger's driver shouted to Stephen as the big black clip-clopped by, eyes rolling. "I wanted to whip that filly of yours once and for all today!"

Stephen made no reply. Leonard Toms, driving Pistol, and Madison Wiles, behind Front Street, gravely saluted with their whips as they passed. Stephen sensed their disappointment that Lady Suffolk would not be trying conclusions with them today. The boy suspected that they both resented all the acclaim that the little gray mare had received and wanted to beat her soundly to put an end to it.

Then Stephen noticed Lady Suffolk. Her ears were up and her nostrils were flaring. It was clear that she was eager to race, but just as clear that she could not—on three legs. Stephen started to take her off the track.

"Gentlemen," the starter shouted through his megaphone, "turn your horses and line up on the pole horse!"

The four entries turned for the word and came pounding up the track toward the judges' stand, vapor jetting from their nostrils, eyes bright—four abreast.

"Go!"

The crowd exploded in cheers. Stephen's chest was swollen with emotion and the blood was rushing through his veins. He felt the same sense of frustration in Lady Suffolk. She turned her head, and she and the boy looked at each other. Then she put her right forefoot down.

21

ONE DOWN AND
THE OTHER COME ON

The pain was excruciating. Lady Suffolk had a roaring in her ears that had nothing to do with the crowd. Waves of nausea swept over her, and she looked through a red mist that grew steadily darker. The searing torture that came like flames from her right forearm seemed to envelop her entire body. The roaring grew louder, the nausea more demanding. The mist was almost black.

Then, down in her forearm, she felt something pop, and a warm wetness ran down her leg. Almost immediately, she had blessed relief, as the abscess drained. The roaring in her ears stopped. The nausea passed. She blinked and the mists cleared. She had already started forward in a flying trot.

Now the roaring was, "Lady Suffolk! Lady Suffolk!"

She and the boy set off in a stern chase. They had lost nearly thirty seconds, and the field was approaching the quarter post. The race was hopeless, but she and her driver did not know that. With Stephen leaning forward and the mare's head stretched out, they tore after their opponents.

"Lady Suffolk! Lady Suffolk!" The cheer sounded like a gale.

Trotting smoothly, squarely, her legs clipping off the distance between her and the others, the little gray mare began to come up on the field. To encourage her, the boy was singing:

> She's a mighty gray horse
> Oh, she is, yes, she is,
> She's a mighty gray horse
> That can sleep standing up,
> And can trot all day long!

In the back stretch, the dust thrown up by the other horses swept into their faces, nearly blinding them, but Lady Suffolk continued her long, low-sweeping, locomotive drive and Stephen went on singing.

Up ahead, Pistol led the field by a length and a half, followed by Hussar, then Jolly Roger, with Front Street in fourth place.

Hussar and Jolly Roger began to come up on Pistol. Madison Wiles touched Front Street with the whip, and she leaped forward. A light chestnut with a white mane and tail that switched back and forth, the pacer swung both left legs out together, then both right legs, so that she had a rolling motion, like a ship in a heavy sea. But she was traveling, coming up on Jolly Roger, passing him, coming up on Hussar.

The closer Lady Suffolk and Stephen drew to the field, the thicker was the dust engulfing them. Blinded as they were, they nevertheless kept reducing the distance between them and their opponents.

At the third quarter, Front Street passed Hussar and began to come up on Pistol. Jolly Roger and Hussar were neck and neck. On the turn, coming into the home stretch, the black's sulky swerved wide, as usual. The right wheel grazed the left of Hussar's sulky. The big roan rose up on his hind legs, then plunged forward, running rough-gaited.

"Lady Suffolk! Lady Suffolk!"

She was still coming up on the four other horses. Pistol still led, but Front Street was pressing him. Jolly Roger was a close third. In the home stretch, Lady Suffolk drew near Hussar.

Stephen saw the startled look in the eyes of the roan's driver. Lady Suffolk saw the same expression in the eyes of the roan as his "breakfast" passed him. He was still running rough-gaited. One of his forefeet flew up and kicked away the pad on his belly.

"Lady Suffolk! Lady Suffolk!"

She kept coming up on the other horses . . . and coming up and up on them. With a furlong to go to the wire, Pistol still led, although Front Street had narrowed the distance to a length. Jolly Roger was a poor third.

Hoof by hoof, Lady Suffolk cut the daylight between her and the black, but he was still nine lengths ahead. With two hundred yards to the wire, she had reduced his lead to eight lengths.

"Lady Suffolk! Lady Suffolk!"

She heard this, but, even clearer, she caught the voice of the boy:

> She's a mighty gray horse
> Oh, she is, yes, she is. . . .

Jolly Roger was six lengths ahead . . . five. She could see his crazed eye as it rolled back at her. One hundred yards to the finish. Four lengths. Three . . .

Crossing the finish line, it was Pistol first, Front Street second, Jolly Roger third, and Lady Suffolk fourth, trailing the black by a length. Hussar had caught his trot but he still came in dead last.

The presiding judge and his two associates, a trio of bearded men in top hats, checked their watches and conferred. Then the presiding judge took the slate that hung outside the stand, wrote the winning time on it, and put it back in place:

2 min. 33 sec.

The crowd cheered. That was only one and a half seconds off the record that Pistol and Front Street shared.

Between heats, Stephen kept Lady Suffolk closely blanketed and moving, except when he was rubbing warm liniment on her legs. The Culleys and Jerry Bean hovered nearby.

"Never, sir, have I seen such game and bottom," a man told Culley.

"Truly, her feet were flying so fast I expected them to strike fire and set her blaze, truly I did!" another exclaimed.

Culley's chest swelled.

"She's in splendid speed and wind," he remarked to Jerry Bean. "I've never seen her so full of ardor and determination. I'll win this meet yet!"

*   *   *

The drivers drew lots for the second heat. Hussar got the rail; Front Street was next to him, then Pistol and Jolly Roger, with Lady Suffolk on the outside.

The starter called the horses up to the mark. He was leaning out of the stand as the five opponents turned around and charged toward him neatly, in their post positions.

"Go!"

The five sprang forward. Even though Hussar had the best position, Pistol shot ahead and by the quarter had edged over to the inside. Hussar was not trotting well. His driver, a tight-faced, muscular man, was leaning way back, pulling hard on the reins. The pad had been replaced on the roan's belly band, but he soon kicked it off again, and, almost at once, cut himself deeply.

The little gray mare and Stephen slipped over toward the rail, behind and to the right of Hussar, so that they were trotting through the flying drops of his blood. As in the first heat, she came up on Hussar, came even with him, and started to pass him.

His driver was whipping him steadily, meanwhile hauling back on the reins. There was a sharp explosion. The pressure of the driver's feet against the iron bar had made it snap. Hussar broke his stride, did a double break, and was out of the race entirely.

At the quarter pole, it was Pistol by a length, followed by Jolly Roger, with Front Street third and Lady Suffolk fourth. At the half, it was the same. In the third quarter, Front Street passed Jolly Roger, and Lady Suffolk started to come up on him.

"Keep your distance, Tecumseh!" the black's driver

yelled, flogging his horse desperately. "Beware, you filthy redskin! I'm going to get you before this day is out!"

Because of the roar of the crowd, Stephen couldn't hear the warning, but he could read the man's lips. Then he kept his eyes forward, as Lady Suffolk passed Jolly Roger on the turn and set off after Pistol and Front Street.

Coming up the home stretch, it was Pistol and the chestnut neck and neck. Then the pacer pulled ahead.

And that's the way they went under the wire: Front Street by a nose, Pistol second, Lady Suffolk third, and Jolly Roger fourth. Time: 2 min. 34½ sec.

As Stephen was rubbing Lady Suffolk's legs with liniment, the Culleys and Jerry Bean came over.

"Papa, didn't you have something you wanted to say to Stephen?" Meg asked.

"Yes, Trouble. 'Better is a little with content than much with contention.' "

"Papa!"

"Stephen, if I win today—"

"Papa!"

"Okay, Stephen, whether I win or lose today, I want you to drive Lady Suffolk in all her future races. And I'll give you a fifth of all her earnings."

"Papa!"

"A fourth, I meant to say, a *fourth!* I'll have a contract drawn up Monday morning. Okay?"

"Yes, sir," Stephen replied with a grin as they shook hands on the agreement. "Okay."

"She's all there, Stephen," Jerry Bean told the boy. "No matter that she's been beaten twice. A race like that second heat took as much out of the other horses as it did her, and you can see she's not discouraged, that she's ready to come again."

"Yes."

"I expect from now on she'll start to tire, and she'll break if you don't use the bit like I told you. Just a half-turn of the wrist, like this."

"Like this."

"There's still considerable trot in her," Jerry Bean said.

"Considerable."

There *was* considerable trot in those gray legs. Lady Suffolk's pipes were open, she was breathing well, and her blood was booming through her veins. But she was beginning to feel the effects of a week of inactivity and of being off her feed.

For the third heat, her post position was slightly more favorable than before. Pistol had the rail. Jolly Roger was next to him, then Lady Suffolk, with Front Street on the outside. Unable to get his sulky repaired, Hussar's driver had been forced to withdraw the roan from the race.

At the word, Pistol took the lead and held it to the quarter pole. Then the others began to come up on him. He fought them off going into the back stretch, but by the time they came to the half-mile pole he had begun to fade and all three of the other entries passed him—first Jolly Roger, then Lady Suffolk, and then Front Street.

In the third quarter, Lady Suffolk and the chestnut began to edge up on Jolly Roger. The big black's driver ignored Front Street, directing all his attention to Stephen and the little gray mare.

"Keep that filly out of my way, redskin," he yelled, "or

I'll run you both into the ground!"

Lady Suffolk and Jolly Roger were trotting nose to nose, matching each other stride for stride, with Front Street coming along on the outside. Lady Suffolk's hoofs felt big, heavy. She couldn't get enough air, and fatigue was settling upon her.

"Beware, Tecumseh!" Jolly Roger's driver yelled. "I'm going to have that yellow hide today!"

Lady Suffolk was lightheaded with weariness. Her legs were beginning to stiffen. The sulky behind her felt like the butcher's wagon. Her ears twitched.

Stephen saw this and, with a half-turn of his wrist, shifted the bit in her mouth. At once, she became alert, refreshed, going on with her fine, square trot.

Jolly Roger's ears twitched, but his driver didn't see that, concentrating as he was on Stephen. The big black reared up and came down in a bad break. Lady Suffolk and the boy quickly left him far behind.

Stephen edged the little gray mare over to the rail, and Front Street followed. As they approached the drawgate, Lady Suffolk had the best of it by a half-length. Madison Wiles gave Front Street the whip, and the pacer leaped forward, her white mane flying.

She came up on Lady Suffolk. A hundred yards from home, her nose . . . and then her eye . . . and finally—fifty yards from home—her ear was level with the little gray mare's shoulder. Wiles was whipping the pacer steadily. She broke, and Lady Suffolk won going away.

The presiding judge and his associates conferred, comparing watches. The top hat of one wobbled as he shook his head unbelievingly. Then he took the slate and wrote on it, with a shaky hand, the time:

2 min. 29½ sec.

After that, about the only three men at the course who were not bareheaded were the judges. Hats flew off by the thousands, like massive flights of ducks, blotting out the winter sun. The women were waving their handkerchiefs, kissing everybody in sight, and crying a good deal. The men were shaking hands and slapping backs. And everyone was shouting.

"Incredible!"

"Do tell!"

"She broke the world record!"

"For mercy's sake!"

"Huzza for Lady Suffolk!"

"It's a feat with no parallel in the history of horseflesh!"

"There must be some mistake. No horse in all the creation could go that fast!"

But there was no mistake, as the following heat proved. Lady Suffolk drew the rail, led the field all the way, fighting off Pistol, then Jolly Roger, and finally Front Street, winning in two minutes, twenty-eight seconds.

Men in the crowd glanced about, looking for a hat to toss into the air. The women still had their tears. But there was not the jubilation that followed the record-breaking heat. The cheering—what there was of it—was muted and was quickly choked off. People gazed at Lady Suffolk and then at each other in awe, aware that they were sharing an historical event. A hush fell over the crowd.

Waiting for the fifth and last heat, Stephen kept Lady Suffolk blanketed and rubbed her legs with warm liniment, talking or singing to her the whole time. When the drivers drew lots for their post positions, Jolly Roger was on the rail. Next to him was Front Street, then Lady Suffolk, with Pistol on the outside.

Summoned forward, the four drivers turned their horses around and came down the track toward the judges' stand. The starter was leaning out, straining to see as the contestants trotted toward him abreast.

"Go!"

The four horses dashed forward, pelting down the track toward the quarter pole, the hoofbeats and rattle of the wheels loud in the strange hush that still hung over the crowd.

"She's a mighty gray horse. Oh, she is, yes, she is," Stephen was singing.

In a tight cluster, the contenders went into the first turn, sulkies twisting, skidding, wheels throwing up a great cloud of dust. Lady Suffolk had her second wind and had never trotted better, but she was boxed in. Jolly Roger was in the lead on the rail. She was directly behind him. Pistol was on his outside, and right behind the Spanish horse was Front Street.

The frustration was acute. Time after time, an opening appeared, but, before the little gray mare and the boy could take advantage of it, the hole closed in.

As the field approached the half-mile post, Stephen gave a gentle tug on the bit, and Lady Suffolk slowed her trot. Their opponents dashed away, leaving them lengths behind, as she and the boy pulled out to the center of the track. Then Lady Suffolk lengthened her stride, pouring out her energy, hoofs going squarely and in line with the smooth, regular drive of pistons.

Nearing the turn at the three-quarter pole, Pistol was ahead, closely pressed by Front Street, with Jolly Roger third. Eating their dust, eating up the daylight, the little gray mare and the boy raced after them. They caught Jolly Roger on the turn going into the home stretch.

They saw the black's sulky coming out toward them— they were thirty feet from the rail—coming at them through the cloud of dust its wheels threw up, skidding, sluing, getting closer each moment. Lady Suffolk saw the mad eyes of the black. Stephen saw an equally mad look in the eyes of his driver. In a few seconds, the other sulky would crash into them.

Stephen gave a half-turn of the reins. The bit moved in the little gray mare's mouth, giving her the extra stimulation she needed, and she spurted forward, quickly outdistancing Jolly Roger. The black's sulky continued to skid— his driver had no control now—and they crashed through the outer rail.

Jolly Roger fell, screaming, with a badly wrenched leg. His driver heard the scream, mingled with the cries of horror from the crowd, as he hurtled through the air, and those were the last sounds he heard for a long while.

Edging over toward the rail, Stephen and Lady Suffolk completed the turn and started up the home stretch. Pistol was still in the lead, with Front Street a couple of lengths behind.

The boy and the mare had a furlong to catch them, just two hundred and twenty yards. Hoof by hoof, they came up on their opponents, passing Front Street a hundred yards from the finish line, then closing in on Pistol.

The Spanish horse and Leonard Toms fought them off frantically, but they would not be denied. With fifty yards to go, Lady Suffolk and Stephen put a length between them and Pistol. Then here came Front Street.

The boy and the little gray mare saw the pacer's smoking nostril coming up fast on their right, as Madison Wiles and the chestnut made their final bid. For forty yards, the two horses raced side by side like a team, Lady Suffolk in her square trot, Front Street in her rolling gait, neck and neck, head and head. Then, in the last ten yards, Lady Suffolk inched forward, winning by a nose.

As in the previous heat, the cheering was muted, the people keenly aware that they were playing a part in racing history and watching that history unfold in awe. When the judge wrote the winning time under those of the other four heats on the slate and hung it in place, there was a gasp:

2 min. 29 sec.

Not once, not twice, but three times in a row, Lady Suffolk, the little gray mare from Long Island, had trotted the mile in less than two and a half minutes. It was, as the people kept whispering to each other and to themselves, incredible. The match today, as they kept repeating, had to be the race of the century.

After he reined her in, Stephen jumped down from the sulky and went up to the little gray mare. Putting his arms around her neck, he spoke softly into her ear.

"You have earned a long, long rest, Lady Suffolk," he told her. "Stephen Seven Tree's Montauk intuition tells him that you will have to wait a long, long time before you get it. But, at least, he will be driving and you'll never feel

a whip again. That is a promise. You are going to win many more races, and you will lose many more, too. But Stephen Seven Trees knows as well as he knows that the sun will go down soon and come up again tomorrow morning that you will always do the best that's in you because that is the way you are, and you will never, never, never change."

Then he climbed back into the sulky, and he and the little gray mare made their way through the awed crowd to the winner's circle.

The Author

John T. Foster has worked as a reporter on newspapers in Florida, North Carolina, Louisana, and New York. He has always been interested in horses, and has to his credit an Associated Press award for a series of news stories he did once on a heroic little quarter horse.

A native of Chicago, Illinois, John Foster is now a technical editor for the New York Ocean Science Laboratory in Montauk, New York, at the eastern tip of Long Island, where he lives with his wife and young son. He also has two grown daughters.

His books for children include *Marco and the Tiger, Marco and the Sleuth Hound, Marco and That Curious Cat,* and *The Mississippi: Ever-Changing Wonderland.*

The Illustrator

Sam Savitt's illustrations have appeared in national magazines and in over ninety books, some of which he wrote himself. He lives with his wife on a small farm in North Salem, New York, where his favorite pastime—when away from his drawing board—is riding and schooling horses.